# Undisput

*He's looking for his destiny, she's looking for a new beginning, only not for herself—but together can they make both their dreams come true?*

Nicholas McDermott had been a lost boy with no place to call home until he was sent to the Sunrise Ranch. There he became part of the dream of Lydia McDermott before she died, the dream of taking a child who had no one and giving him a home, a family and a place to come home too. Now, he is a success in the business world and has decided it is time to give back, if he can just figure out what his calling is. Whatever it is he knows it's in Dew Drop Texas, now, he's bought his own ranch across from his family ranch and all of his brothers and knows when it's time he'll know exactly what his destiny is… and hopefully he'll find a partner in life and love like his brothers' have been doing lately.

Emmy Swanson has started over in Dew Drop with a clothing store that make her enough income to enable her to bring her injured, younger sister to live with her in her small home and give her a new life since she almost lost hers saving Emmy.

Now, surrounded by wonderful people including founders of Sunrise Ranch and the boys of the ranch, Emmy feels she is where she's supposed to be. What she isn't expecting is the handsome new rancher in town who takes her breath away and throws her heart in to a rampage when they meet. She has no place in her life for dating much less testing the waters with a man who causes more chaos inside her heart than anyone ever has.

**But then, she hears Nicholas is thinking about opening a rehab ranch, a place to help those who need it find their way back to strength and agility through the help of horses... could this be the answer to her prayers?**

**Don't miss this heart thumping addition to the Cowboys of Dew Drop, Texas you might just fall in love...**

# UNDISPUTABLE COWBOY

Cowboys of Dew Drop, Texas, Book Five

# DEBRA CLOPTON

Undisputable Cowboy

Copyright © 2023 Debra Clopton Parks

# CHAPTER ONE

Anticipation raced through Nicholas McDermott's heart as he stood on the hillside overlooking the ranch he now owned.

These acres of pastureland splattered with and array of oak, cedar, pine and mesquite trees in various areas was going to be enjoyed by his cattle, *his* cattle—he smiled just thinking of the cattle belonging to him.

This ranch now belonged to him, and that made his smile grow.

He was home. And he had a plan.

More than the livestock would appreciate this land; he had a vision for it. Not yet totally defined in his mind, but kids would benefit from this beautiful place—of that he was certain.

He was on a mission and there was no doubt in his mind that when the right mission was clarified to him, he would recognize it.

What he knew was this ranch would benefit kids—*how* was the question.

The amazing Sunrise Ranch had been that for him, as it had been for all four of the jean clad men standing beside him, his brothers, not of blood but of heart. He turned to look at them.

The McDermotts—Morgan, Rowdy, and Tucker, the original brothers who, because of their amazing mother's dream—had added many, many brothers to their name, including him. He was blessed to be one of them in heart and mind, because they'd, as a family, embraced their beloved mother's dream of making the ranch into a foster home for boys like him and Chet, who also stood with them overlooking his ranch.

They all stood together as brothers because Lydia McDermott's dream had been fulfilled by her husband, Randolph, and her mother-in-law Nana. Because of *her dream* they'd all come a long way together, and now, here they stood like the brothers they were.

Lydia, the mother and dreamer, had died too soon to see her amazing, huge ranch become home for boys like him. Boys with a need for love, family and a place to call home…a place to let go of their anger and pain from their previous life and to start over.

And so, Sunrise Ranch had become a safe haven for him and other boys, like Chet—guys who'd never had the love that her sons had from her, their dad Randolph, and grandmother Nana. But they not only found those dreams at the ranch, they'd found hope, too.

Lydia's sons had been suffering their own grief at losing her, and he and Chet some of the first boys to arrive had watched these three men deal with their broken hearts. Unlike them, these guys had known how deeply they were loved. They'd learned love doesn't always last, because a body doesn't have the ability to hang on when it's overcome by some terrible illnesses or tragedy. Life wasn't fair in those ways, and Nicholas had learned that.

They'd *all* had to overcome, in their own ways, the cards of life they'd been dealt.

As good as life on the ranch had been he'd been

driven to become a successful businessman. He'd realized after college that he had the ability to buy a failing business at a rock-bottom price, save it, and sell it for far more than he'd invested. And so he did. And the sales got bigger, and so did his bank account.

However, with all the money, something was missing.

Never had he acquired the fulfillment that he sought.

Finally, it slammed into him that he could build it, buy it, and have it all—he'd thought it would be a payback to the two who had tossed him away—but making big bucks didn't bring him fulfilment like he'd thought it would.

He realized he wanted something more, and that was when he'd started thinking of moving back home to Dew Drop. Now, here he stood with his brothers.

"What do you think?" he asked.

Oldest brother, Morgan, always the serious one, gave him that look. "You're going to make something great out of this." This man took life and made it what he wanted, which was to make life easier for others who hadn't been blessed the way this ranch had blessed all of them. With his father and grandmother Nana, he had now joined in and was determined to continue growing his mother's dream.

The other brothers did their share, too, helping run the big ranch and teaching the boys the skill of ranching. And through learning, all of them—like Nicholas had done—would be able to one day make their own dreams come true.

*Now,* like them, he was going to make his life count in more ways than money and self.

"That's my plan," he said. "Giving back something of what your mother's dream did for me is my goal. That's why I asked y'all to come today. I have this idea about helping kids and young adults with needs, not just orphans, but kids who have a disability in some way. Physical disability or mental disability because, as we know, many of our brothers lived through worse than others before coming to Sunrise Ranch. We all know horses helped us overcome and can help others too. So my thought is instead of an orphanage, I can do a camp where kids or anyone, actually, can come for a week or two weeks and get help or be inspired by being on the back of a horse. Learning to ride—with help, if needed, to be on the back of that horse."

"Great idea," Rowdy said, and Tucker and Morgan nodded agreement and waited for more information.

"I look at the great actor Paul Newman and his Hole In The Wall Gang Camp, where children with serious illness can experience the thrill of life and just be kids. It's inspiring. He's made a humungous difference in the lives of those children all across the world. Like Sunrise Ranch has touched our lives, he's touched lives in a different way.

"And now I'm seeking my way to make a difference. I'm thinking I could use horses to help those who need it. Using this land that we all love so much to help them recover from mental or physical issues. I believe it would be something that the woman I'm now blessed to call my mom, Lydia, the woman you three had the privilege of being born to, would smile down on me and give me a thumbs-up. So I'm asking, what do you all think of this idea? You too, Chet, because you've figured out how to give back in the way you do."

All four of his brothers smiled, their eyes and expressions serious as he met each one with his questioning gaze.

Tucker was the first to speak. "I can see you doing this. And you're right, Mom loves it. She's probably looking down from heaven and smiling that amazing smile of hers." This was a military hero who knew what sacrifice was. He lived now, because a young man they all called brother had followed Tucker into the military and stepped in front of him and given his life to save Tucker. He'd dealt with it and now he served as sheriff of Dew Drop, Texas, after coming out of the military. But he was still there for all the other boys when needed and sometimes for a roundup. He was always there as someone to look up to. And Nicholas was one of those.

Rowdy grinned. "My mother would have loved this idea." Rowdy McDermott was one vibrant, happy cowboy. Through his trauma, he had found the beautiful, wonderful Lucy, who had lived through a bad fire and a marriage that was hard. Now they, too, were happily married and were perfect for each other.

Nicholas had run with this guy for a long time; it was as if they were two of the same mind. They had both had their wild sides and they had both figured out that that wasn't going to make them be the man they wanted to be, so seeing that shine in Rowdy's eyes gave his heart an extra-hard thump.

Rowdy continued, "I'll help in any way you need me."

Morgan nodded. "Same here."

"I agree," Tucker added.

Their agreement was all he needed. But he had to look at Chet, who had yet to say he thought it was a good idea.

Those thoughtful eyes were serious, but his smile dug deep. "I can tell you, as a kid who survived the wreck that killed my parents by clinging to a bush in rabid rapids until some great man came to that water and rescued me, I had a mass of anger trapped inside me. I found what I needed here finally at this ranch on the back of a horse. Being on a horse's back, can work miracles. I know because my anger was deep; I couldn't let it go but being a horse helped. It wasn't just riding out my anger on the back of a horse, letting loose and running full throttle across the land that helped me. It was feeding and taking care of them that helped too.

Then my remarkable April came into my live and was the final key to my happiness.

"But this idea about horses helping those who need it, to find the comfort they give us when we touch them and ride them…" His smile grew, and it touched Nicholas deep inside because that was the difference the two of them had lived through that linked them. "*God's* going to use you, brother. I think it's a brilliant idea, and I'm here for whatever you need."

Looking at them, his heart pounded hard against his chest, and he knew this was going to be his payback for all he'd received from one woman's dream, to hopefully help others like he had been helped and continue the legacy.

He smiled big, huge all the way from his heart. "All right then, this is *going* to happen."

\* \* \*

Emmy Swanson walked out of her store, Jeans And Things, the store she was so grateful for here on Main Street in Dew Drop, Texas. The wonderful town she was about to finally bring her little sister here to call home.

The town Emmy had found after a trauma in her life had set her on a path to finding her own way. And that of her sister—her sister who had almost given her life to save Emmy. The sister she was determined to start a new life for in this wide open-armed community of wonderful people.

She'd been mistaken as someone's granddaughter from church when she first came to town, and it had taken a little while to let people know she wasn't related to anyone in Dew Drop. She was just the woman who'd come out of nowhere and opened her store in preparation for when she could bring her seventeen-year-old sister here to their new home.

Determined to help her sister as soon as she could come live with her, Emmy had researched towns that had reputations for making a difference. And she'd been drawn to Dew Drop, Texas. The little town was closest to Sunrise Ranch, the wonderful ranch that housed sixteen orphaned boys at a time. A new child was brought in when one left to start his adult life. Some chose to stay here, but most of them found life for themselves and came home for visits to their family at the ranch. Recently, she had watched one cowboy find happiness, and she had helped his new bride find a new outfit. It had been fun and had helped Emmy know she had chosen the right town.

She was headed to the Cow Pattie Café—well, that wasn't actually the name of the diner; it was the Spotted Cow Café—run by heart-lovin' Miss Jo, who was an amazing pie maker. But she also had a fun sense of humor, and the diner was decorated with all manner of spotted cow paraphernalia. Including the floor, which had spots painted on it. Spots that were supposed to represent a milk cow's black spots. The funny Chili Crump and Drewbaker McIntosh, the two men she could see sitting ahead of her on their town bench, had nicknamed the diner the Cow Pattie Café. Needless to say, they had at first infuriated Miss Jo, but the woman had a great sense of humor and had adapted to it and let it go.

Now sometimes people said Cow Pattie and sometimes they said Spotted Cow Café, just like she did. They were the same, and both brought smiles to her face. Today she was meeting several ladies there for coffee and to tell them what was about to transpire in her life. Actually, none of them knew that she had a little sister who had been in a physical rehabilitation center off and on, and then, after their horrible ordeal, been placed in a foster home until now, until she'd reached the age that she could choose where to live.

And that was with Emmy, who had diligently worked to prepare the home and the finances that would help make her sister's life easier in a town of the most loving and giving people she'd ever been around.

There was Miss Jo, the owner and amazing pie cook at the café, and her crew inside the diner—T-bone and Edwina, the waitress she adored. Then there was the lovely lady who owned the wonderful Dew Drop Inn, and their friend Nana, the amazing lady who was the grandmother to all number of young boys and men who had come through the gates of Sunrise Ranch and now called it home. Today, they were all having lunch because this was a gathering of ladies getting ready for the yearly Family Reunion Fair, where they hosted a gathering of all the boys who had become men while Sunrise Ranch and Dew Drop were their home.

They held it here in town and at the ranch, and everyone loved it. She had moved to town right after it was held last year but heard it was a wonderful event. Now, she was excited she would get to meet so many of the men who had been raised here. Boys who'd been through trauma and were safe now, something she was familiar with—not that anyone knew this about her, but this had been another reason she was drawn to Dew Drop. The support, the love, the examples that these people set to help all these boys become strong men was inspiring.

And the women of town were too. The women who fell in love with these men she'd come to know, like her, had backgrounds that were rough also, but they'd overcome it and found love too. Not her; she wasn't looking for that but hoped that her sister found it one day. Rainy deserved the best and someone who was strong and gallant and would love her to the moon and back. Just the thought made Emmy's heart swell with hope.

Her heart ached as the pain that sometimes swept in suddenly for what her little sister had suffered trying to warn Emmy that she was in danger. In doing that, she had been hit by the truck aiming for Emmy. She'd almost died but lived, then had to endure much recovery time and hard work to be able to get around with the walker that was her full-time partner now. And Emmy was determined to make a wonderful home for her sister. Her little sister who had suffered so much for her and because of her—the last part she shoved away, not needing to go there just yet. She was stronger now and had learned that sometimes you had to speak up, take a stand, and ask for help.

Now, her focus wasn't on her past mistakes but on making sure she did everything in her power to help her little sister walk again. To have a great life full of love and joy.

She just had to figure out how. But she knew if anybody could help or care about her sister, it was these ladies who had hearts as big as Texas. She took a breath and headed down the sidewalk.

*Get a hold of yourself,* the voice in her head said. The voice that urged her forward, the voice that refused to let her lie down and cry that day, the voice that demanded she stand up and fight.

And she had done just that. And her life had changed forever…

What she'd done was slam the door to her heart to anyone other than her cherished sister. She'd never regretted the actions she'd taken against the man who had done the dirty deed. She'd saved her sister and to her that was what she was meant to do.

Then, she'd moved forward in order to prepare for the day she could give her sister her new life. She'd researched, determined that Rainy would recover and live a wonderful life in this beautiful little town, and these ladies would help.

And these men. She smiled as she reached Chili Crump and Drewbaker McIntosh, the two locals who had nicknamed the diner the Cow Pattie. They sat on their bench, carving like they loved to do. It was always fun to see what their new creation was for the day. Retirees, they kept up with everything, knew everything, and had an unforgettable way about them.

They both stopped carving their creations as she approached them. Their grins appeared and widened in welcome.

"Hello. How are you two busy men this morning?"

Chili hitched a brow. "We're good. But I hate to tell ya, it's not morning, it's lunch time. You going to meet the crowd?"

She chuckled. "I guess it is. And yes, I am meeting the lovely crowd today."

Drewbaker patted his knee with a red toned, wooden bird he'd been carving. "They're all in there, getting ready for the gathering. We told them we'd come in and help them, but they told us to sit out here and decide what kind of mishap we were going to create for them to fix." His lip hitched upward. "Like we're hazardous or destroyers, which we're not. We just like coming up with something fun for the annual gathering."

She smiled wide at them. "I think they're going to have that fishing tournament that they always have, and I heard y'all like to fish out of a large metal watering trough."

Chili grinned. "Yes, ma'am. We have it, but we haven't used it since we did that one year. Now we use a regular boat. But that's an idea. We'll have to check it out and make sure it's still going to float. We've aged a bit, and I personally don't want to have to swim in the lake. What do you think, Drewbaker?" "I don't like to swim, period, but I can if need be. I do like to fish and catch the big ones and well, our good buddy Walter Pepper, who helps run the ranch out there. He told us that Wes is coming home." He grinned. "Wes has always been really helpful to us, and he joined in on rolling that giant trough down the hill. Since he is a mighty bull rider now, I'm sure he's even stronger than he was when he helped us a couple of years ago with it. So, this might be a good thought."

These two mischievous retirees eyes danced at the thought. They gave some of the ladies a hard time she'd heard and it looked like they were both contemplating it now.

"I'd love to see you two in the metal watering trough. And Wes…I know his name, but I've never met him. He sounds like a good guy. So I'm looking forward to meeting him. But, right now I better get in there to the meeting because I've got something important to tell the ladies."

She started to walk past, and Drewbaker patted her hand with the bird and she paused. "Anything we need to know? Anything we can help with? You look kind of serious suddenly."

She sighed, knowing she might as well tell them too. "My little sister, who I haven't talked about much since I moved here, is finally able to come live with me. She's been in a foster home since she was eight after a terrible ordeal. Now she's reached seventeen and I get to bring her here to live with me in the home I've made for her and the town picked for her. Dew Drop is a great place for her to start her, *our* new life together."

"That's wonderful," Chili said. "We'll be glad to meet her."

Drewbaker studied her. "We sure will. I'm sorry y'all got separated but glad you are finally able to reunite. Is something going on, you look stressed out suddenly?"

They saw all, it was true. "We had a hard life, and our age difference was hard but now we can forget life before and move forward. But I've gone most weekends to visit her, making sure we've been a part of each other's lives. Rainy was injured and put in rehabilitation then foster care. She's better than she was but uses a walker. I wish she could walk like she didBut at least she's able to come live with me and we can continue her rehabilitation. I'm on my way into the diner to let everyone know about her. I know she's going to love it here."

She held back from saying more than she needed to.

As she'd talked both men had sat up straight, as if on alert. "We're here to help," Chili said. "If she's in that pretty little dress store with you and she wants to come out here with her walker and see us on this sidewalk, we'll teach her how to carve."

"Sure will," Drewbaker agreed. "We'll do whatever you need us to. Believe us, we have many men we love who had to overcome stuff. Had to overcome sitting in a wheelchair and some had to learn to live with it. Some were able to walk again but not all of them. You can count on us to help." He smiled and handed her the bird. "This will be her first gift. And I just have to tell you,

you did good choosing this town to bring her to live. All these people are great and all those boys from the ranch, they've all overcome or they're getting there. It's rough, sometimes, you know, but we as a town, we've bonded together to help those who need us. *So*, I can guarantee you that you can count on that."

Her heart squeezed tight; tears swelled in her eyes as she took the bird and held it in her hands. "Thank you. This will sit on the shelf—no, on the bedside table. She will see it every morning when she wakes up, and I'll tell her exactly who made it for her. Maybe she'll be curious enough to want to learn to carve. It could be helpful for her. I've been searching for what would be the most helpful to her, so thank you, you've made my day."

"We're here for her," Chili said. "Now, go on in and let the ladies know. They're going to be there for you too."

Her heart warmed with their words as she smiled, then walked toward the diner.

Her sister was going to do well in Dew Drop. Emmy had made the right choice.

# CHAPTER TWO

Nicholas pulled into the parking space and saw two of his favorites, Drewbaker and Chili, two men who had just retired and taken their seats on the sidewalk right before he left for college. They'd loved this town so much and through the years, he had heard that through their fun-loving spirits, they had inspired more than just him. He didn't get out of the truck because they were talking to a beautiful woman, and it looked like they were having a deep conversation so he didn't want to interrupt them.

He wondered what they were talking about and who she was. When both men straightened up on the bench, not relaxed at all, and their expressions turned to ones of determination, he knew some serious conversation was taking place. The warm brown hair of the woman moved as she hugged the carving against her, then walked away toward the diner's sunny-yellow door. Both of the men watched her leave just like he was doing, only seeing them in his peripheral vision. He yanked his gaze away as she entered the diner through the big, bright door. His gaze went back to Drewbaker and Chili as they looked at each other and started to talk.

Nicholas got out of his truck, closed the door, then headed their way. He had to pass a new ladies' store with a lot of bright clothes in the window. Pretty stuff like the teal-toned blouse the lady had on with her white jeans and tan ankle boots. The woman probably shopped at this store. He kept walking; he wasn't looking for women's clothes, not yet anyway. Maybe one day, if he found someone to love him, this would be a nice place to shop for a gift.

Before he reached the older men, they spotted him, and their serious expressions changed to wide grins as they both stood up. He walked straight to them and threw an arm around each man's shoulders. "Hey guys, it's great to see y'all," he said as he gave them both a hard side hug. They'd done this to him many times over the years.

Chuckling, they both gave him a light fist to the belly while he continued to squeeze them tightly. They all laughed before he finally released them.

"It's about time you showed yourself in town," Drewbaker said. "We heard you'd come back and bought that big ranch across from Sunrise."

Chili's eyes twinkled. "We *heard* you're trying to figure out what you're going to put in out there. Any ideas? We'd like to finally hear something from you, out of them grinning lips of yours."

It was as if no time had passed, and they were meeting every day here on the sidewalk near the entrance to the Cow Pattie. That was the way it used to be, and the way he looked forward to it being from here forward.

He hooked a thumb on his belt. "I talked to the guys just the other day but haven't been to town until now. I was unpacking and getting things in order. Whatever I do will involve horses. Riding a horse can be a miracle worker in someone's life—was in mine and a lot of my brothers' out there on the ranch. So, doing physical therapy on a horse is on my heart and mind. What do y'all think?"

The duo's gazes met, then Chili was first to speak. "I think it's meant to be. It's a perfect idea. We both know how good you are with horses. We know how talented you are on one. The fact that you made such a success out of your life and it had *nothing* to do with horses startled us."

"Yup, it did," Drewbaker agreed.

Chili continued, "However, you deciding to come back here and get back to what you're really good at could mean far more than those millions of dollars you have flooding your bank account. I like it. Like it a lot."

Nicholas grinned at that. Not the money part—which was true—but it was the coming back home, doing what he was good at that caused the smile. He was home.

Drewbaker grunted. "Yup. I agree with him. The timing is perfect."

Both men nodded. Their eyes turned back to serious as they drilled into him.

"The timing? Is there something you know that I don't know? I mean, is there somebody you know who needs something I can help with?"

They looked at each other as if he were giving them a problem they were torn between. Finally, Drewbaker nodded at Chili.

Chili cleared his throat. "I'm going to tell you this, but we just learned it ourselves and right now, all of those ladies in the diner are learning it. Did you see that pretty lady standing here beside us?"

He nodded and said nothing, because Chili barely gave him time to nod.

"That's Emmy Swanson. She's a really nice young lady who moved here last year. Matter of fact, right after we had our big gathering, she opened that little ladies' clothing store. Everyone likes her but no one has really gotten to know her because on Fridays she leaves her store to her helper and heads out of town. She doesn't come back until late on Sunday evenings, as far as any of us can tell—those of us who pass her little house coming into town, that is. So, basically, she's never here on the weekends."

"Okay, so what's wrong with all of that?" He was baffled.

Drewbaker gave his buddy a glare and took over. "She just stopped by to talk to us and told us all this time she's been going to see her *little sister*. Her sister who has been in foster care for some reason and walks with a walker. She was hurt when she was younger and is still recovering but finally old enough to leave foster care. So Emmy is bringing her here to the new home she has created for her. Isn't that great, Emmy chose Dew Drop to make a home for her in our town. But the poor girl was hurt really bad and still has healing to do."

Nicholas was stunned. The timing was like a thump to the head telling him this was the right move.

"Stunned us too," Chili said, as if reading his mind.

Drewbaker reached out and grabbed his shoulder. "Yeah, when you hear the Lord's voice, it's kind of startling, isn't it? You think that might be something you need to listen to?"

Okay, so they *could* read his mind, but that was nothing new. These two had eyes that seemed to look in and see everything. Of course, they sat here and talked to everybody and listened to everything spoken within hearing distance, so they pretty much *did* know everything.

He looked toward the diner and wondered how this beautiful lady found this perfect small town that would embrace her and her sister. He knew for a fact that this town, these people, would give her everything they could to help her. And her sister still needed healing— the exact words he'd been waiting to hear. Now here he stood with the dream in his head turning into a real possibility. He might be the one who could help.

"Fellas, thanks for filling me in. If you don't mind, don't talk about what I just told you. I've got to get some things figured out first, so just in case it falls through, I don't want to get anyone's hopes up. Not that this lady has asked but just in case she were to hear something before I know. It might not matter at all but let me get more figured out." *Was he worrying too much?*

Drewbaker patted him on the shoulder again, then dropped his hand to his side. "Go on in there and have you some of that good lemon meringue pie that Miss Jo makes. Get involved in that conversation that's going on. It might be good, and then too, not that I'm a matchmaker or anything, but that is one fine gal and she's about your age."

*Wow.* He looked at the two mind readers. "Okay, fellas, I'm going in but let's not go to the matchmakin' talk. When I'm ready to find someone, I'll do the looking. So, call off that thinking right now. You two have a good day and thanks for the heads-up." He walked away but not before he saw the two give each other that look...the "he's interested" look.

*No, not going there just yet.*

# CHAPTER THREE

Emmy's heart thumped against the beautiful gift and those two good-hearted men's words for her sister. She'd opened the door of the Spotted Cow Café and was greeted instantly by the mooing of the mechanical cow, alerting everyone she'd arrived.

She smiled. The place was so entertaining, with all of the funny cow displays hanging from the walls, ornaments, plaques, and singing cow clocks. Everything imaginable hung on the walls. And on the floor, there were blobs of black paint representing spots of spotted cows. Everything about this place made her smile. It was a hoot and she loved it.

But not just the décor. There was the owner, Miss Jo, who had walked out from the kitchen the first time

Emmy walked through the door, and she'd seated her, then placed the coconut pie in front of her. It had been her *delicious* welcome to town.

And now here stood Edwina, the unique waitress who had a gruff voice and a stern look, but behind all that camouflage was a heart of gold. "Howdy," she greeted Emmy. "You go on over and find a seat with the ladies, and I'll get you something to drink. You just tell me what to bring ya."

"Thanks, you're awesome. I'll just take a glass of lemon water—I mean water with lemon." Her nerves had shaken her words up and got a grin out of the unique lady.

"I could try to get some water in a lemon, but I think the other way will be better. Good luck." She leaned in and whispered, "They're really into it. This is going to be one special reunion we hold, you know. All those kids are going to enjoy it, then everybody's coming back. Don't tell them, but I always enjoy it myself."

Emmy smiled as Edwina headed to get her drink. Yes, she had a gruffness about her, but a sweetness that was most of the time disguised with that crustiness.

Now Emmy focused on her reason for being here and headed toward the group at the tables in the back area.

"Come on in here, pretty girl," Miss Jo said as she came through the swinging doors from the kitchen. She carried a pie in her hands as she headed to the table.

Knowing she was about to get a piece of the pie that was beneath that beautiful topping of meringue, Emmy followed the wonderful baker and owner of the Spotted Cow. They weaved through the tables toward the table of grinning ladies. There was Mabel Tilsbee, who owned the historical Dew Drop Inn, a wonderful lady who was really good friends with Miss Jo. The two ladies were the inspiration for this little town and meant a lot to everyone. And their buddy was Nana McDermott, the cofounder of Sunrise Ranch with her son. All the ladies enjoyed getting together. Mabel often went on special trips to help families hit by disaster in other countries and sometimes here in the United States, dealing with a tornado or hurricane aftermath.

Mabel loved doing this, and Emmy valued that about her. It was one of the things that had drawn her here, because her little sister was going to need all these amazing people.

In the booth sat Jolie McDermott with her wavy red hair and her beaming eyes. She was a wonderful person. She'd been a championship kayaker who had given it up to marry Morgan and be the teacher of all the wonderful boys at the ranch. She, too, was a reason Emmy had chosen this town. Jolie had overcome things in her own life; she was an achiever through good and bad, and that was what she needed her sister to be.

Beside Jolie sat small, blonde Lucy McDermott, who was married to Rowdy. An amazing artist, she wore a beautiful soft blouse that surprisingly didn't come all the way down to her wrists and exposed some of her scars on her arms. There had been a time that no one would have known that on those arms and on her body were scars. She'd hidden them from everyone but now she had no fear of people seeing them. She had learned here in this amazing town that people didn't look down on her because her body had been damaged. No, she was a survivor and, again, had inspired Emmy to come here.

And across from Lucy was Suzie McDermott. She owned the florist shop in town. She was married to

Sheriff Tucker McDermott, another one of the McDermott brothers.

They all had had wonderful lives and lived through a lot, and unknowingly embraced her when she first came to this town before she had decided to open up her shop here. She had driven here and checked the town out, ate here in the diner, and stayed at the Dew Drop Inn. It was like a gift from God, her having heard about this place. And something deep in her heart told her this was where to make her new home.

Told her this was the place where Rainy and her broken body could find what she needed. And so, she bought a small house just outside of town in case Rainy wanted to stay home some days and Emmy could leave the shop and check on her if needed.

Everyone was smiling at her and welcoming her as she came to a halt.

"We've got you a spot saved right here." Jolie patted the chair between her and Mabel.

Emmy sat. "Thanks. I'm happy to be a part of this wonderful get-together this year."

"We're glad you're a part of us now," Miss Jo said.

"It doesn't take a lot of planning anymore because everyone likes what we do every year. They love coming to town for the food and games, then heading to the ranch for some rodeo events and sometimes a fishing tournament."

"It sounds enjoyable. What are some of the things you do?" she asked. Though she'd heard some of the fun things before now, she wanted to see what her sister might be able to do.

*And you need to tell everyone,* the voice in her head pushed her.

Jolie grinned. "All the boys enjoy both places. One of their favorite things is throwing cow patties."

Everyone laughed, and so did Emmy. "I'd heard that. Never seen it but it has to be an experience."

Lucy chuckled. "Oh, it is. They all compete, young and old. Winning that cow pattie trophy is the top of the list."

She laughed, thinking about it, and knew her sister would get a kick out of it.

Jolie grinned. "I see that smile. What are you thinking about?"

*It was time.* "I just was thinking about the cow pattie trophy sitting on a shelf in the house. And I heard someone say the champion bull rider from here won it last year and is carrying it around with him in his horse trailer on his travels."

All the ladies chuckled. Miss Jo, cutting up the pie—lemon pie—looked at her and grinned. "That's Wes. I love that boy—well, I love them all, but that is one strong young man. And those stout bull riding arms of his threw a long, hard drive of a cow pattie last year. Kind of set a record. Obviously, his bull-riding muscles helped him throw that thing. He'll be here the day before the gathering, and the guys are anxious to see him and Joseph."

"They both mean a lot to the boys," Mabel said. "So, this is about more than tossing the cow patties."

"That's right," Jolie agreed. "Over the years, when the guys come through the ranch, they connect…they're all brothers, but they connect really tight with the ones who are living at the ranch when they are there. And those two young men are strong encouragers and well loved. Maybe you've met Wes when he's been visiting?"

"Maybe. But I'm not usually here on the weekends, so I feel like I haven't."

"Then you're in for a treat. Joseph, too." Jolie smiled, and Emmy saw the love in her eyes as everybody talked quickly about how excited they were to see everybody who was coming.

Emmy listened, taking it all in as she tried to determine when to tell them about Rainy.

Mabel nudged her. "You're going to have to get involved in some of these activities, especially that three-legged race. You put your eye on some of the cowboys in town to race with. Maybe that cute one over there." She nodded toward a couple of men sitting within view. "He's got his eye on you, and he's a good guy. He'll be there, so if he asks you, maybe take him up on it."

*She was trying to be matched up.* "Mabel, that's thoughtful, and he does seem to be nice, but I have something to tell all of you." That got everyone's attention. So she let her gaze take everyone in. "The reason why you don't see me on the weekends and why

I don't date and won't date is…"

Everyone was zeroed in on her now, and she knew why. Early on, they'd asked her why she left town on weekends, and she'd said she went to see family or was clothes shopping for the store—which was true sometimes. After it became her way every weekend, they'd stopped asking, but now she saw curiosity in their gazes.

She smiled. "I have a little sister. She's seventeen, and the nicest girl you'll ever meet. I came to Dew Drop because I picked it for her."

"That's wonderful," Miss Jo said, speaking for everyone. "But why hasn't she been here before?"

She told them what she'd told Drewbaker and Chili. "She's in foster care, but also was in rehab for a long time for injuries she sustained when she was about eight and was in a wheelchair. Now, she's able to use a walker with wheels, and she still has a little way to go before she can, hopefully, walk again. That's a great hope and maybe a long shot. She may forever be on her walker, which at least gives her the ability to stand. But, no matter what, I chose this town to have a wonderful life in. I visited here and saw how wonderful y'all are and how much all the boys from the ranch love it here, so I chose y'all. I chose each and every one of you ladies, not that I'm going to hold you liable."

She gave them a soft smile. "But I know my sister will feel the love that lives here among you all. I'm going tomorrow to pick her up and bring her home. And I'm hoping to find some way to help her build the strength she needs to walk again."

As she spoke, the cow mooed at the entrance, but all eyes remained on her. And there was compassion glowing from everyone.

Miss Jo spoke first. "Darlin', we're going to welcome your little sister with open arms. I'm not going to ask—only if you want to tell us—what happened to her. But if it has taken her this long to recover, we're so thankful she's able to come here and become part of our everyday life. You can bet she's going to get as much of my pies as she wants."

Mabel touched her arm. "I knew from the day you checked into my hotel by the way you looked at this town that meant something. After you moved here, I thought you had been studying it for that dress clothing store. But then your weekend trips had my curious side spinning. But we learned we have to earn the trust of those around us before we learn what matters most to them. And, darlin', you can trust each and every one of us sitting at this table. We're going to be here for you and your sister."

Edwina stepped forward—obviously she had been standing behind her—and she placed her water beside her. "I'm tellin' you, you did right pickin' this good town. I'm kind of known for runnin' folks off if they don't act right. If they come in and harass anybody, I'm going to send them on their way. And I promise you, I'll be watchin' out for your little sister. I have a feeling she's going to be coming to stay with you at the store some. If she wants to come down here and spend time at the café, you let me know, and I'll come walk her down here. I'll look out for her."

She almost teared up. Edwina was offering to be her sister's protector. That made her heart swell. "Thank you."

Lucy leaned out from her booth and patted the edge

of the table with her small hand, the burns on her wrist and forearm showing. "You did right. When I came here, so scarred and hiding underneath my heavy shirts and long sleeves…well, this was the town that helped me heal. These people and my tender-hearted Rowdy. So, we're glad you're doing this. I'm actually excited. I can't wait to meet your little sister. And if she wants to come out to the house and learn to paint, you bring her. She's getting here in time for the town celebration. It's going to be awesome."

Tears welled up; they'd been trying to escape and now they licked down her face.

Suzie reached across the small space between her chair and the booth and patted her arm. "Tears are okay. I know that there may be some sadness there for whatever put your sister in this situation but there's also joy. You came to the right place. For me, with my son Abe, I came here so desperate, trying to find him help, trying to find the right place to help him heal after losing his daddy. And this was it. This is a healing place, a fun place, and a place where dreams come true. Don't you forget that. We're all here for you. We're glad you chose our wonderful town."

In her side view, she had seen a tall, lean cowboy sit in the booth right behind them. He had looked at the menu but now he lifted his head, and it drew her attention. Her tear-glistening eyes met his vibrant, strong, cinnamon eyes.

"I'm sorry," he said in that moment. "I got here and heard your private conversation, but my name is Nicholas McDermott. I'm one of the boys who call Sunrise Ranch home, and I just moved back to town. I'm starting my own ranch here, and I have to ask a question. Do you think your sister could ride a horse, with a little help?"

Heads turned from looking at him to looking at her...

*Could her sister ride a horse?*

# CHAPTER FOUR

Her insides jumped like she was springing on a trampoline. "I don't know. I...I wish she could. I don't ride horses, but I wish I could too. My little Rainy was always more adventurous than me, and before her...accident, she could beat people at anything she put her mind on. She could run fast, climb trees, swing from a tree on a string...though she was young, she was a free spirit." She sighed and looked down at her now clutched hands. *If only her sister could do things like that again.* Something about the quietness around her had her lifting her gaze. Everyone had glistening eyes as they looked at her, and her heart clenched tight at the sympathy.

She wiped her tears and said in a quivering voice,

"Y'all are going to love her. Because even though she's relying on a walker right now, she's still got a spirit that even tragedy couldn't stop." Her tearful gaze met the man who still watched her.

His eyes glowed with determination. "Then you just helped me decide with certainty what I'm going to do with my new ranch."

The man's soft, firm, and determined words touched her heart. As her eyes met those golden-rimmed cinnamon eyes, she was intrigued. "What do you mean?"

"Nicholas," Miss Jo said. "We're excited you're back in town. We all knew there was something up, and now we really want to know what it is."

Everyone echoed Miss Jo in a flurry of questions. And even from the tables not in the group, their words drew attention.

The rough-looking cowboy who sat one table over spoke up. "Nicholas, you were always an adventurer, always a dude who knew what you wanted and pushed yourself hard. Everyone in town knows you're turning properties and dead companies into gold on reselling, so

I'm really curious about what brought you back to town after all of that money that you're making."

His words had Nicholas's gaze going to the guy, and he nodded. "You're right, Larson. Even though I had the wonderful love of this Sunrise Ranch and of my Dew Drop family, I had to prove myself to myself, and I did. But something was missing as I did that. Proving to myself that I wasn't worthless as my parents thought when they tossed me away didn't fill my heart the way I needed it to. So here I am, back in town, and planning to give back something that was gifted to me through many of these caring ladies sitting here." He gazed at the ladies in the room.

Emmy was transfixed by his words as he continued, and everyone else was zeroed in on his words too.

"You ladies showed me what value is. As did my family, the McDermotts. Nana, you carried the torch of a dream and helped make it a reality. Mabel, Miss Jo…you did the same. And I want to follow in your paths. I just wasn't sure if my idea was the one to go with, until now. Now, I have the confirmation that it was the right idea, so I'm opening a rehabilitation camp."

Gasps went around the room. Emmy held hers in, but it was huge inside her head.

"I can house people for a couple of weeks, or a little longer if need be, to get them on the back of a horse. It's good for people, really is. It wasn't just good for us angry boys who came here."

Her heart thundered at his words, and his eyes didn't flicker from hers. "A rehabilitation camp?"

He nodded. "I think your sister will enjoy getting on the back of a horse. It will help her with her steadiness. 'There are a lot of things that can help your mind, your spirit on the back of a horse. And if you think that's something your sister might like to do, I'm offering her the spot as my first client. You and she can come out there and we'll work with her, do whatever we need to, for free. I'll be making that the aim for most people, but I want to give it to you for helping me learn. So, I'll be getting it going, and the offer is there if you decide you want to take me up on it."

She couldn't believe what the man was saying. Her pulse rate was on high as she stared into those amazing eyes and told herself it was just because of what he was saying. But then there was that little toe of the boot kicking her in the back of the brain because she recognized how gorgeous he was and that was *not* something she wanted to do.

No, no, *no*—it wasn't.

"I think it's a great idea," Mabel said. "Your little sister would probably get a lot out of it just being out there on the ranch and getting up on the back of the horse. She would love it—well, I'm assuming she would since I haven't met her yet. But what do you think?"

*What did she think?* "I think it's an incredible offer. And I'm thanking you very much for it, but I can't set anything up right now. I'll have to ask her. She puts on a good strong show for me, I think, but I can't make that decision for her. Do you understand?"

He nodded. "I totally get it. This is what I'm going to do. I'm going to get started and if by chance your sister doesn't want to do it, I'm going to open it anyway. God used you, Emmy, to give me the green light. You've shown me exactly what I want to do, and now I can guarantee you it won't take me very long to get open. I'm a very determined man."

"Yes, you are." Miss Jo slapped a piece of pie on a plate and walked to his table, setting it in front of him. "And if I remember correctly, this lemon pie is your favorite. You're doing a good thing, and I can assure you that sweet Lydia, rest her beautiful soul, would be proud of you."

Emmy watched the smile spread across his lips and the glistening in those remarkable cinnamon eyes of his were full of emotion.

"Miss Jo, I started my profession out there determined to show the world that I could be who I wanted to be, that my parents hadn't ruined that for me, and I went after it like fire on dry grass. But then, it wasn't satisfying. I realized I was doing exactly the wrong thing. So, your words are right on target. From here on out, I'm doing everything I can to give honor to the *sweet* lady. I never met her, but I owe who I am today to her and to all of you. The ones who carried her dream forward." His gaze touched Miss Jo, Mabel, and then rested on Edwina. "Even you, Edwina. As demanding and straightforward as you ever were, I want you to know you taught me, taught me to watch, then react. To take matters into my hands, and I did. But, again, I was wrong. You don't do it out of a hard heart; you do it because you're looking out for people."

The woman's eyes held his, and Emmy was startled by the intensity in her look. "You learned good."

He nodded. "I know there were times when you looked out for me, and I'm sure you're still doing it for everyone else. I'm not the only one who thanks you."

Every eye had turned to Edwina. The tough as a granite rock stood there, eyes looking straight at Nicholas. "I might have put my foot out and tripped a few wranglers as they ran out of the diner trying to catch you once, but you became strong and stopped running. Believe me, I learned it the hard way because I married three big ole mistakes and finally put my foot down and said no more. Now, I'm free as I can be and always will be because I only do what I want to do. I only smile at who I want to smile at, and right now that's you, cowboy." And she smiled a big, huge smile.

Emmy had never seen her smile like this and obviously no one else had either, from the looks on their faces. Even the big, tough looking Larson looked stunned. But her gaze was drawn to the grinning Nicholas. He stood, took the two steps between him and Edwina, and the cowboy embraced her.

And everybody sitting around them gasped, along with Emmy. And big, gruff looking Larson shifted in his seat, drawing her attention to his disgruntled expression. What was up with that?

Emmy looked back at Nicholas McDermont hugging a startled Edwina. This man obviously thought the world of her, and all these nice ladies. But the fact that he hugged the standoffish waitress and had the woman's tough looking expression melted instantly was stunning.

Stunning not just her but everyone in the diner.

* * *

Nicholas felt kind-hearted, blunt, determined Edwina tremble in his arms at his impulsive embrace. Then, she patted him on the shoulder, gave him a squeeze, and nodded her head against his shoulder. He knew that for her, this was more than likely the first hug the woman had had since he met her all those years ago. Most people didn't realize what this tough cookie of a woman did for everyone. How she looked out for them and how much she probably needed a hug every once in a while. He'd risked getting punched when he'd scooped her up but now, he leaned back and grinned. "I was prepared for a punch in the gut, but I'm glad you didn't give it to me."

She put her hand on her hip. "Well, I decided that I'd rather be hugged by a good-looking cowboy like you, one I helped put in his place a few times." She grinned. "And like you said, helped protect a few times. So, I enjoyed it. But don't go thinking you can hug me all the time. I'm not the woman for you, mister, so don't get your thoughts going in that direction. Just want to warn you so you don't get the wrong idea."

The room busted into laughter.

Edwina put both of her hands on her hips and glared at everybody. "*And* don't y'all go getting carried away. Anyway, now that I got my hug, I've got to go get to work." She turned and started to walk away.

Larson put his boot out in front of her. She halted, placed a hand back on her hip and stared hard at the cowboy who was eyeing Edwina with a big grin plastered on his face.

Edwina frowned even harder at him. "Don't go getting any ideas, dude. Eat your food. It's almost time for you to leave—it'd be better to go now than gettin' on my bad side, and me running you out of here."

Larson's grin widened and suddenly it slammed into Nicholas, was that interest he saw in Larson's eyes as he moved his boot and let Edwina walk on by and his gaze followed her?

*Interesting.*

It was none of his business so Nicholas sat back down and his gaze instantly met the beautiful Emmy Swanson's. The expression on her face was pleasing. It was…what were the right words—touched? Intrigued? She blinked and glanced down at the pie now sitting in front of her. Her chest heaved with a deep breath.

He yanked his gaze back to her face as she looked back up at him with those warm caramel-toned—he loved caramel—eyes.

"I'll be sure and talk to my sister about it," she said. "I'll not push her, but I'll put in a great word for you. Obviously, you're very serious about what you do, and your heart is definitely in the right place."

His heart instantly went on a rampage, and he prayed nobody could see it flopping with the movement of his starch shirt.

*Whoa, what was going on?*

# CHAPTER FIVE

Emmy drove toward her home on Saturday with Rainy, her amazing sister, in the passenger seat. Happiness wasn't a big enough word to describe the feeling rolling through Emmy. They were together again. "We're getting close to our home. Our fresh start."

Rainy turned her golden hair from the window so that her soft, pretty face could be seen. Her emerald eyes held light, which sent joy through Emmy.

"I like it," Rainy said. "I like how it has the flat lands and then every once in a while, I can see those ravines out there in the pastures. If I could walk, you know I'd be exploring them."

Emmy's heart fell. "I want so much for you to be

able to explore like you did when you were a kid. Before all this…terrible stuff happened. But, now you're older, getting stronger, and we're going to do everything we can to help you get further along. Like the people at the rehab center said you could. Everybody in town wants to meet you and encourage you, and a lot of them have stories that are full of hardness they overcame. And *you*…my strong-willed little sister, are going to do it too."

Rainy grinned at her before Emmy put her gaze back on the road. "And you, big sister are wonderful." Rainy placed a hand on her arm, drawing her gaze back. "I'm proud of you."

Her sister's words touched her deeply. Rainy had been born when Emmy was nine, and she had been a beaten-down little girl by that time. But when she saw her baby sister, something inside Rainy began to change. Instead of taking the beatings like she always had, she started jumping in to take their dad's fury on herself so Rainy would be spared. She had lived through her abusive parents—a dad who put it out and a mother who did nothing—but she couldn't—*wouldn't* watch it happen to Rainy.

And she'd made it to to her senior year, almost old enough to hopefully get custody of Rainy when she graduated and reported him. They just had to make it a little longer. She'd be eighteen by graduation and was determined to take her sister away. But then it happened, the day everything changed. She and Rainy were in the yard and her dad weaved the truck into the yard and he and their mother had stumbled out of the truck. Both were drunk.

Emmy told Rainy to go to the hiding place but before she could their dad grabbed her by the hair and yanked her to the ground. Emmy kicked him and he growled, but let her sister's hair go. Emmy yelled go hide to Rainy and her sweet sister ran.

That was the moment Emmy couldn't let it go anymore. The day she'd made her stand and told them she was taking Rainy with her. It had been the day their lives had changed.

Her mother stared with glazed over eyes and just stumbled away. The man who caused all their pain glared at her, then spun, steady enough he went back and climbed in his truck. Relief had surged through Emmy but then, instead of driving away, he'd cranked the engine then stomped the gas and came flying straight for Emmy. She screamed and was about to dive out of the way…but on that day—that day…her brave, furious, tiny sister raced from behind the large tree next to the side of the house and jumped in front of the truck arms waving.

Emmy thanked God for the rain-worn, deep ruts in the drive because the truck hit one sending it slightly to the side and off target. On that day the Lord saved Rainy. She'd been sideswiped instead of hit head-on—death would have been her future but instead she'd been thrown through the air and landed on the pile of old logs.

Emmy had watched and her heart exploded in shreds as she believed Rainy was dead. In those moments anger raged through Emmy like she'd never felt before and she prayed she never felt again. In that moment in time her mind flew into fury—she grabbed the rusting bowed, spike rake lying unused among the trash surrounding their falling-down shack. Her drunken dad blasted from the truck, radiating with fury too and totally focused on Emmy—not the child she'd thought he'd just killed.

Her poor sister crumbled in the logs but he could care less as he rushed toward Emmy waving a tire tool. His fury enabled him to move unbelievebly swift, but Emmy's didn't back away, she swung the pointed, curved rake head and it made contact. He yelled, stumbled and fell to the ground rolling and the pistol in his boot lay between them. Then, like the drunk manic he was he reached for it as she swung again. Then he fell face-forward into the dirt.

Only then had she thrown the rake down and raced to her sister, terrified she was dead. Prayers on her lips, she'd turned Rainy over into her arms and her amazing sister was still breathing and looking up at her with her unbelievable emerald eyes.

Never would she forget that moment—her heart had been overjoyed when her Rainy trembled in her arms—*alive*, and weakly said, "I *love* you."

And from that moment on, their lives had changed for good…they were torn apart but alive and away from the two people who'd shown the the way not to live the rest of their lives. Today was a new day, a wonderful day.

Pushing the past from her head, Emmy drove into a driveway and smiled at the person who mattered. "You're going to love it here in this perfect town. Everyone is excited to meet you, but I hope you're going to love it here in your new home."

"It's perfect," Rainy said softly as Emmy put the car in park and shut it down.

The small but pretty, white wooden house had a tiny yard that Emmy had made certain looked good before she went to pick her sister up. She had mowed with her small mower and planted red geraniums in the front of the beds. Pink roses stood behind the red flowers, the bright colors making the house look happy and welcoming—at least, that was her goal.

Along the walkway, the yellow lantana made a welcoming trail from the carport to the porch. The walkway she'd made certain was even and wide enough for her sister's four-legged walker. It led from the metal cover for the car to the front door, and it also went from that same place to the wide side porch that entered the kitchen door. It was, out of all the homes she had looked at, perfect for her sister and her situation. And one she could afford without spending too much, because she had saved everything she could to have her sister come live with her and be able to help her.

She made certain that the walkway was pretty because it would hopefully be where Rainy could come outside and at least walk from the back porch to the front door, looking at the flowers and getting some exercise in the small area outside the house.

"It's just a small place—two bedrooms, though, and two baths. I put you in the room right beside the bigger bathroom. It isn't gigantic but I made sure to measure very closely, and your walker can move around in there so you'll be able to get in and get out yourself like you've been able to do already. The bathroom in my room is just a shower and a toilet and a sink they squeezed in there, but it's good for me. I think it's perfect for us."

"You've done great." Rainy smiled. "Can we go look?"

Emmy smiled, her heart full. "Yes, come on. Let's

get you inside." She got out, rushed around the back side of her car, popped the back door open behind Rainy, and pulled out the rolling walker—the new one she wanted her to have here. It was steady, and she knew her sister would be safe walking with it.

Now, she pulled it opened and set it in front of Rainy, who had hoisted herself out of the car and now took hold of the handles and immediately started to head toward the low back porch. Emmy was relieved to see how easy it was for her to move along the concrete sidewalk. Her whole thought process, every day of this past year when she had come to Dew Drop and settled, was to make everything convenient, easy for her sister. The doctors had said there was the possibility that Rainy might never walk without a walker because there was a chance that she might never regain the strength in her left side, where her back damage upon being hit and thrown had been worse. Already she was a walking miracle.

But Emmy prayed with time and now complete focus on gaining strength her sister could one day walk with no effort. God had already worked a miracle in her sister's life by just giving her the possibility, and it was something she would never let her sister forget now that she was able to live with Emmy. Until now, she'd been in a foster home. Now she was home with her sister. Emmy smiled down at her sister as she pushed up with her bent arms. She wasn't a big girl, and she wasn't as healthy as she needed to be. That, too, was about to change. Patsy, her foster mom, didn't make them eat—they did, or they didn't. And her sister just didn't eat enough to make her as strong as she could be. At least that was what Emmy thought. She was going to be well-fed here, that was for sure.

Emmy couldn't wait to take her to the Spotted Cow Café. She smiled, thinking about it. "You're looking good. After you see inside the house, we'll go to town and eat dinner. I can't wait for you to go into the Spotted Cow Café."

At those words, Rainy's gaze lifted to hers, and her eyes brightened up a little. "I would like that. But are you sure you want to take me to town? I mean…"

"Yes. I'm absolutely sure. I can't wait to take you to town, Rainy." She placed her hand on her sister's hand gripping the metal handlebars with a tightness that told Emmy there was a fear that dwelled deep inside her sister. "You're going to love it. And everyone is going to love you. I can't wait for you to meet everyone. This will be late in the day, so not everyone will be there. But this would be a good time to go in and see everything. I think Miss Jo will be there, and T-bone will be cooking—and oh my goodness, that man can cook. Miss Jo's pies and cakes are amazing. And then Edwina might be there. She's a wonderful waitress—a little bit different and a little bit harsh, but she already told me that when you're at the shop with me, if you want to come down to the diner and visit, she'll come to make sure you get there okay. And Drewbaker and Chili are offering for you to come out and sit with them and learn to whittle. They are all looking forward to meeting you."

"They sound like wonderful people. And I hope I don't disappoint them. But I am looking forward to meeting everyone." She took a deep breath and smiled. "Let's go inside and let me check out what you've done. You sound so excited about it, and I can't wait. But I will be ready to eat. You hungry?"

"I'm real hungry. And I'm glad to hear you say that because, sister, we're going to eat good tonight. I'm hoping you eat a little bit more than you've been eating because I don't think you've had great food. I can assure you you're about to enjoy the best."

* * *

Nicholas made his calls. He had gone out to Sunrise Ranch to see his brother, and they'd gone together and picked the horses they thought would be the best for his new facility. Before he left, he'd been glad he was there when Wes, their champion bull rider, arrived. Wes had just won the NFR and was all grins as he got out of the truck and looked at them all. He drove miles and miles across the country, going from one rodeo to the next, one competition to the other to get all the points that he needed to make the finals in Las Vegas. Good ole Wes hadn't even hesitated as he'd come over, wrapped his muscled arms around Nicholas, then lifted him off the ground and hugged him hard around the waist.

Nicholas and all the others busted out in laughter.

He slapped Wes, who was his brother through this great ranch, on the shoulder. "Come on, bud. Let me down."

Wes dropped him and, thank goodness, he landed on his feet. "What are you doing here?" Wes asked as everyone laughed.

"I'm getting horses that I can use on my new rehab ranch business."

"Rehab?" Wes asked, his serious gaze locked on him. "You're gonna help hurt kids with horses?"

"Yes, that's the plan. I think it can really help them with the fun and ability that riding horses gives us."

"Yes," Wes said. "The fun that they can have doing that would be awesome. I saw a girl at the rodeo awhile back, and she couldn't even walk but her brother was one of my competitors, and she had come to watch him. While we were all outside before going to get ready, she pulled her wheelchair up beside one of the barrel racers who had her horse beside her, and she asked if she could sit in the saddle. I was amazed and a bit scared for her, so I went over to help. Wow, she might have been in a wheelchair, but she was strong. She looked up at me and all the other guys and said, 'No thanks, I've got this.'

And she had, with her own hands. Her brother watched and grinned, because he had obviously known what his sister could do. We all watched in amazement as she used the saddle, gripped it, pulled herself up out of that wheelchair, and then she pulled herself up onto that saddle, with her chest hanging over and then reached over with her right hand and grabbed her leg and yanked it over that horse, then pushed herself up in a sitting position. Then, she used her hand to put one foot into the stirrup and then the other and there she sat. She had use of her body, everything but her legs. It was amazing. You should have seen the smile on her face, the determination. She rode that horse and didn't take sympathy from anybody. Kind of threw me for a loop.

"You know, I've been out here on this ranch my whole life, trying to ignore the anger inside me, you know, and helping my brothers through all their hardships. But I've never been around a girl who was as full of determination as me and who was happy. I know there's people like that, but I've just never been around them. Come to find out, she was getting married. And her future husband came up—you should have seen that man…he was one long, tall cowboy—and he got over there, and she grinned down at him. She was happy to see him, and she happily slid into his arms from the top of that horse. And, well, I'm no romantic but that was cool. Anyway, would you be looking for anybody to help you?"

Those words had been exactly what Nicholas had needed. Wes was mentally powerful, emotionally powerful, and physically powerful enough to help anyone on and off a horse he was perfect for his special ranch. Nicholas felt God had given this cowboy the experience he'd had so he'd be ready.

Nicholas's grinned as he drove into Dew Drop to have supper with Wes. He never had thought Wes was going to be happy always on the road, riding one bull after the other. Something inside this young man drove him to want to help people in some way. Wes was like Chet, who had known he would never leave the ranch because his heart was here on this ranch. He was devoted to the boys, helping each of them learn to live here and make this ranch home and to mentally leave behind whatever they'd been through before arriving here.

But, like him, he had come back here with this dream that he hadn't known exactly what it was, only that here, following in the footsteps of his founding mother's dream, he wanted to do more. And he had a feeling that Wes would be driven for something more too. He wasn't going to put all his hopes on Wes, but he just had a feeling and hoped this was going to be something that Wes was really good at and had a heart for.

He got out of his truck just as Wes drove his truck into town and pulled in beside him. Wes was full of energy and, thank the good Lord, still had all of his movement because he'd never been injured in his fight to become a champion bull rider.

Wes was still one strong cowboy, and now he barreled around the end of the truck and just hopped up onto that sidewalk, stuck his fist on his hips, and grinned at him. "You coming?"

"Yup. I ain't going to jump up there like you did, but I'm coming." He stepped up onto the sidewalk just as a small SUV pulled into the parking lot in front of where Drewbaker and Chili usually sat morning to afternoon. They had already gone home at this time of day. Nicholas's heart did a slam against his ribs as he realized Emmy was in the driver's seat of the SUV.

The woman had been on his mind since he last saw her here in the same spot, except he'd been the one in his truck and she'd been talking to the whittlers. Now, everything in him instantly focused on Emmy. The beautiful, caring woman whose sister he wanted to help.

He yanked his thoughts off of Emmy and refocused on helping her sister—where it should be at this time. He had something he could offer to help that young woman and he would do it. And then he saw the young lady in the passenger's seat and figured it was her sister. They had come to dinner at the Cow Pattie, too, and as he stared, her gaze met his—just as Wes elbowed him.

"That is one pretty lady."

"Yeah, she is. But don't be making any moves. She's a little older than you, and I can already tell you she's only got one thing on her mind."

*"You?"*

*"No,* man." He almost laughed but deep down, he

wished maybe she did. But no, her mind was focused on her sister. "Her sister," he said, as she opened her car door. "Her sister is who I'm hoping will be my first person to help out there on the ranch. I haven't met her yet, she's just come to town today, but she's unable to walk without a walker—"

"Well, let's go help." Wes stepped forward without hesitation. The tough-looking cowboy strode down the sidewalk just as Emmy closed her door and was about to hurry around the back side of the low-riding SUV. She didn't say anything to him as she focused on opening the back door of her vehicle.

Wes hopped from the sidewalk and rounded the car. "Hello, ma'am. I'm Wes, and I can get that walker out for you."

And before Emmy said anything, Wes stepped in front of her, reached inside the car and pulled out the folded-up walker, backed up and set it on the ground, spread it out, and smiled.

Nicholas was amazed when Emmy gave a gentle, beautiful smile to the younger man. Before she said anything, he said, "Wes is going to be working with me.

We're brothers. Wes was young when I was leaving, and he joined the brotherhood out at Sunrise Ranch. He's a great fella."

"Wes, I haven't met you, but I've seen you when you've been in town this year, visiting around town."

The front door of the SUV opened, taking all of their attention as the pretty teenaged girl looked out at them. "Y'all going to stand there and talk, or will somebody roll that walker to me?"

Emmy started to grab the walker, but Wes was already pushing it to her. "I've got it. And something tells me just from the sound of your voice that you're one tough cookie who's going to grab hold of this thing and not need my help."

The girl looked up at him and then, without saying a word, she grabbed the two handlebars and lifted herself to standing position—well, not full standing; she leaned hard to one side but she stood as best she could. It was evident that her thin arms were strong because she didn't falter.

Emmy took over. "Rainy, this is Nicholas. He owns a ranch here in town. And this is…"

"I'm Wes. I'm Nick's little brother, and I'm coming off the rodeo circuit and excited to help with the new endeavor he's taking on at his ranch. When I heard he was going to help people like you learn to ride horses like I did when I was a kid, fully strong enough to do it, I was in. I loved riding horses and then bulls. They have both helped me through a lot, so you're going to love it. I can tell you, it will help you."

The look on her face told Nicholas that nothing about his place had been discussed.

"What are you talking about?" Her soft question had a firm edge to it, and her gaze went from Wes to Nicholas and then to her sister.

"I didn't say anything yet," Emmy said. "He just told me about it, and I just brought you to town for supper. I didn't know we were going to be intercepted."

Nicholas couldn't help but smile. "We didn't mean to interrupt y'all's first dinner together since you've arrived. But let's just say when you and your sister talk, then we can talk some too. Right now, let's head to dinner. Wes and I will sit at our table and let you two enjoy your first dinner at the Spotted Cow Café."

Wes put his hands on his hips and grinned. "I'm going to leave you alone once we're inside but right now I'm going to hold the door for you—if you don't mind." The girl had a look on her face. It was not one that was…well, it just wasn't one he could read real good.

"Well, I hate to say it, but you holding the door would be good. That's not something I can do real well with both my hands on this walker. Tried it once and ended up on the floor and never tried it since." There was grit in her words and frustration.

Emmy's gaze met his, and he gave her a nod and hoped his expression told her he understood what she was dealing with.

"I can guarantee you that with Wes opening that door for you, there won't be any falling down going on. So first we have to get you up onto that sidewalk."

To his surprise, Wes grinned. "If you just push that walker down here on the pavement, I've got something in the back of my truck that will get you up on that sidewalk. Of course, if you'd let me, I'd pick you up and put you up there. But I have a feeling since we barely even know each other that's not something you're going to want me to do, so come on…walk with me."

And the boy started to walk, and the girl started to push her walker with her crooked step and bent back, and walked beside him. Wes, the usual Wes who adapted everything in his life to help the boys at Sunrise Ranch, now altered his pace to hers and shot this pretty lady a grin. She didn't smile, but she didn't frown either.

# CHAPTER SIX

Emmy's nerves were rattled as she watched her sister walking beside the handsome young man—*bull rider*, her brain corrected. Wes was a bull rider. Why that kept rolling through her brain she wasn't sure, except maybe it was the fact that he took chances. As she watched her sister pushing her walker beside the bull rider, she couldn't figure out whether it was a good thing or a bad thing. But she could see the kind look in his eyes when he looked at her sister. It was obvious that this wasn't his first round with trying to help someone, and her heart eased as she glanced at Nicholas.

*Nick*, Wes had called him. Both names fit him, but for some reason she liked Nick—not that she was going to use it. He was studying her. "He seems like a young man who likes to help."

Nick nodded. "Yes, always. He has been through a lot in his life, but he made a success of his life through the drive and determination that he has. And I think I see some of that in your sister's eyes. He probably does too. I had a feeling that she might get a lot from this horse riding therapy. If you decide it's a good idea."

"I'm sure we're going to talk about it, because I think maybe I did hear interest in her voice."

They were a few steps behind the others as they reached the truck. "Then we'll talk about it later." Then he strode forward and looked in the back of Wes's truck just as Wes did, and then grinned at him.

"What do you think?"

"Perfect," Nick said. Together, they lifted a wide metal plank from the bed of the truck.

She looked at her sister, and her sister had this look of wonder on her face. "You carry that in the back of your truck?" Rainy said, a hint of laughter in her voice.

Wes's smile widened. "Well, I rodeo, and I never know, you know, when my horse might need to take it easy getting out of the trailer, so I carry this in the back of my truck. Turns out, it comes in handy."

Emmy couldn't believe it. Rainy got this look on her face that said wow—just like Emmy was thinking. Her sister was about to walk up a cattle ramp, and she didn't look upset about it. "I think it's meant to be." She looked at Wes with a smile blooming across her own face.

The two cowboys—handsome cowboys—placed the plank on the sidewalk and the ground at a nice, easy angle, and without even hesitating, Rainy started up it without asking for help. Emmy took it as a good sign, a sign of determination. She did, however, notice that both Wes and Nicholas watched her carefully from their places behind her. They did not try to help or interrupt as she made it to the sidewalk.

Once there, she turned and looked down at them. "Thank you. That worked perfectly. I never thought about myself being a cow, but I guess this crazy piece of metal in front of me kind of puts me in that category."

"No," Wes blurted out.

Emmy caught a twinkle in her sister's pretty eyes, and that twinkle touched Emmy's heart.

"Don't worry. I'm not getting offended by your statement—"

Wes looked serious. "I can tell you've got the determination of a mama cow trying to get herself up into a cattle trailer to get to her baby."

"Well, not that I'm a mama cow, but I am determined. And before we go in and I sit down for dinner with my sister, I want to let y'all know I'm interested in riding horses." She straightened herself up as best she could. "I think it would be cool in my condition to get on top of a horse's back, in the saddle. My arms are strong—it's just my legs that are weak, and my hip."

"It's your heart that matters," Wes said. "As long as your heart is in it, your strength will be too. And we can do it as the strength everywhere else builds."

Emmy's breath caught watching the two kids, young adults, hold each other's gazes. And then her gaze locked on quiet Nick, who had stood there and watched everything come out in its own time. He winked at her. And her heart did a somersault—a stinking somersault. Something she hadn't done since she was a kid. Hadn't planned on any of this happening again, but her heart…well, it did it anyway.

"I think this is a good time to go inside. You two can sit at your table and talk about what you need to talk about, and me and my sister will sit at our table and talk."

Wes smiled. "I think that is a great plan. You just let us know what the timing will be. We'll be working with the horses soon to get them ready. So, we're up for it."

She watched as Wes jumped onto the sidewalk and opened the door of the restaurant. The little cow that stood at the doorway let out a bellow of welcome.

Her heart was doing multi-flips now because for some reason this felt right.

\* \* \*

Nicholas felt good as he and Wes held back as the two ladies walked into the diner. The little scraggly mooing cow that stood at alert and announced everyone's entrance into the diner bellowed a few times. The small gathering of supper-goers looked up and said hello as the young woman on the walker walked inside.

Dew Drop was a welcoming small town, and he was glad to be home. He and Wes, both behind the ladies, lifted their hats hello to all the couples at the tables, though their attention and their smiles were on the ladies. Out of the back came little Miss Jo, hustling and grinning.

"Well, hello, hello. You, sweet girl, must be Rainy. I'm Miss Jo. Your sister told me you were coming to live with her. I can only tell you that we, as a town, are excited that she chose our little Dew Drop as the place for you to become a part of."

"Thank you. I'm glad to be here. And hello, everyone. I'm Rainy Swanson, and this is obviously a fun place to eat." She grinned at Miss Jo, who reached out and patted her arm.

Again, Emmy knew she had chosen right. "Thanks for the welcome, everyone."

Miss Jo winked at her. "Let's get y'all to wherever you want to sit. Are y'all altogether?"

Emmy did not miss the tilt of Miss Jo's voice—

curiosity, she figured, because everybody knew she had never sat at a table with a man here anywhere in Dew Drop. "No, we're, uh, separate tables. But we thank them for helping us get inside."

"Yes, uh, me and Wes have some catching up to do, and I believe these two ladies do too."

Miss Jo smiled, but Emmy didn't miss the speculation in her eyes, and she wondered whether her face said more than she wanted it to.

Miss Jo led them to a table near the window where they could each take a chair and the walker could sit beside it. While they were sitting down, she watched as Nick and Wes walked to the opposite side of the diner and took a booth next to the window. She noticed that Nick chose his spot first, which was facing away from her. She wasn't sure whether she was happy about that—yes, she was glad that he chose not to keep her in his visual.

As Wes slid into the booth like a young man with plenty of agility, he took his cowboy hat off and nodded at her. She nodded, too, and then focused on Miss Jo.

"Well, ladies, I'm going to give y'all a few little

minutes to figure out what you would like to eat. But what would you like to drink?"

Emmy let her sister go first, knowing what she would ask for.

"Can I have a root beer?"

Miss Jo grinned. "Yes, ma'am, you can. Good ole root beer—I love it too."

"And I'll have a glass of ice water with lemon, please."

"And I knew that's what you were going to order, my dear. Should try the root beer sometime. Your sister knows a good thing."

"I know but the sugar gives me some things I don't like, like muscle aches and pains—" She chuckled. "And a pound or two."

"Well, honey, you're doing just fine, believe me, but I totally get the aches and pains. That sugar will do it if you get too much."

Miss Jo walked off, and she looked at her sister. "So, what do you think about this cute cow diner?"

Her sister was looking around at all the cattle on the wall, and as she looked past Emmy's shoulder her gaze

DEBRA CLOPTON

paused, her eyes flickered, and Emmy thought she'd caught a view of Wes. She wondered if their gazes had met? In the next second, Rainy yanked away and went back to the wall on the far side of the room.

"I like that dancing cow hanging on that pedestal over there…the one hanging on the wall. There's a whole bunch of cattle on these walls. It's like going in a place and looking at the wall and trying to decide just how many things you can buy or accumulate to go on a wall—cows, that is. That's all there is."

Emmy chuckled. "And most of them are spotted, like the Spotted Cow Café…goes with the title."

"Yeah, I get it. I see the spots on the floor, too. That's a really cute idea, I think." Her gaze met Emmy's. "I think I'm going to really like this place. You did good. I mean, really, I'm so glad you chose to move and take me with you."

She reached across the table and placed her hand on her sister's. "I told you the day I could get custody of you and the day you were okay to come with me that you would be."

"I know, and I believed you. Patsy was a nice lady.

She tried but she had no time or ability to give me everything I needed. But at least she gave us a home and tried to make it happy, better than the first one I went to."

Oh, her sister was so right about that. She had survived the truck and the long hospital stay and then the rehab center, and then she had had to be put in foster care. That the first foster home really didn't have the want to take care of her. And that was when Emmy tried on their visits to get her sister to push herself because her foster home didn't seem to be doing anything except taking the money from the government. Rainy missed her appointments unless she took her. And she couldn't always be there because she had to work in preparation to figure out how to give them a life that could make them happy.

Then, after she complained strongly, the foster home didn't want her anymore—thank goodness—and they moved her to Miss Patsy's. There, though, it was a large house full of kids. Miss Patsy didn't have the ability to help her sister with much, but her sister liked that place much better and put her foot down and said no more rehabilitation. She was tired of it, and in her heart of hearts didn't think it would make a difference; she was where she was.

The words rang hard, like a slap to the face to Emmy, and it was on that day she decided she would make a difference. She started working hard, working overtime to save every penny she could. After a few years, she knew it would be only two years before her sister was going to be the age to come home with Emmy. So she started her searches, determined to find the perfect town to make their home.

She would buy a hotel ticket, and she would go after work on Friday, drive wherever it was in Texas she was visiting. She'd arrive and spend the night and then take the morning and the afternoon checking everything out before she would head home to be ready for work again on Monday or Sunday night, depending on what her shift was that week.

She worked at a clothing store and felt she could open her own when she found the right town. She'd looked for almost six months, and then she happened to read an article about Dew Drop. After she read that article, the next weekend she headed to town and fell in love. Thus, after walking the streets and seeing no dress stores and knowing that surely every town with women needed a clothing store, she made her decision.

\* \* \*

Wes cupped his hands on the table, his gaze going past Nicholas.

He saw the look of concern in his younger brother's eyes as they paused and then looked back at him. "What are you thinking?" Nicholas asked.

"I'm thinking I want in. Seriously, I knew I wanted in to seek something more, but now I know for sure."

"I get what you're saying, and I'll be so happy to have you helping me for the summer or for whenever, but your expression tells me there may be something more that you're thinking about."

"Yeah, and I'll tell ya, but here comes Edwina." He stood up, grinning. "Edwina, give me a hug. It's good to see you." And without waiting for Edwina, the off-putting, hidden-hearted lady, Wes threw his arms around her and hugged her tight.

Nick grinned; he couldn't help it. He wasn't the only one who loved her. Wes was one cowboy who just did what he wanted with exuberance and he was going to be great at camp.

Edwina grinned as he let her go. "Well there, little boy, it's good to see you too. But don't go gettin' any ideas. I don't date boys as young as you, so you best just sit back down and save that hug for someone your age."

Wes sat, grinning up at her. "Well, I tell you what…if you find somebody you think might match me up, you go with it…show me the way. But I'm interested—are you finding anybody to make a match with you?"

Edwina patted the order pad against her palm and frowned. "So, tell me—when you were on your last bucking bull, did you get your head slammed against the fence or something? You know good and well I'm not really looking. If I was, well, since all the other fellas around my age who live here—you know the McDermott brothers have all married—I guess my next in line is this handsome hunk sittin' beside you. And I don't know, but so far, he hasn't, you know, winked at me or anything like that, so I'm not sure."

Wes grinned at him. Nick smiled and looked up at Edwina. "Well now, I hadn't really been looking, but if you're interested—"

"Hold on now. You just moved back. I gotta make sure you're something I really, really want. Just 'cause you're one of the handsomest cowboys I have ever seen, it doesn't mean that we're going to, like, get started on a romance."

Wes was almost laughing as he slapped the table, probably drawing the attention of everybody in the diner. Edwina wasn't grinning, which was usual; she looked at him with frank eyes, like a challenge.

"Okay then, I guess that puts me in my place, so you just, uh, move at your own pace, and I will too. Right now, if you don't mind, I could sure use that today's special."

Edwina patted her thigh with her order pad. "Well, I didn't even tell you what today's special is...I got sidetracked by this Wes guy here, this cowboy."

"Well, I don't know what it is either, but I know it's

always good, so just throw it in there for me."

"Okay. Today it's raw liver and onions."

Wes chuckled. He looked at her. "Okay, well, if that's what it is, then I'll just have a hamburger."

"Then a burger it is, since that's actually what's on the special. You get it with some of those amazing homemade onion rings that T-bone creates back there."

"Sounds good to me."

"Me too," Wes said.

Edwina snapped her pen to the paper—like she needed to write it down. Then she nodded at them. "Now y'all get back to your conversation. It looked like y'all were seriously involved in something." And then she turned and moved away, headed toward the table where Emmy and her sister sat.

After Edwina walked away Nicholas's glaced over his shoulder and his gaze landed on the warm brown hair of the beauty sitting with her back to him and his pulse instantly sped up. He looked back to Wes.

"Yeah, those two, they make me know that there's more to life than just riding a bucking bull."

Wes's serious words struck a chord inside

Nicholas. "Yeah, it does. There's a story there. Not sure exactly all of it, but I can say that I've offered our help. Not that they're going to take us up on it, but the offer is out there. And I just need to say that one thing we have to be careful about in this business—I expect that since I already know you're a good guy that you'll respect being friendly but keeping your distance." He had to make it clear that romance and what they were fixing to get into was out of the question. But the look in Wes's eyes told him he didn't need to go there.

"Look, man, when I look at that young lady, I see somebody I can help. I'm not interested in romance right now. Believe me, I was blessed to be put here in Dew Drop at Sunrise Ranch, and I've made my life what I want it to be. And I really didn't understand that it was here. That my destiny wasn't riding bulls but helping others who had been put in hard situations like I've been through. I took my anger out on the back of a wild bull, and I was again blessed to be very, very good at it. But part of that was my determination to prove myself. But even after winning all I won in my first two years out, I found no real satisfaction in it. My satisfaction comes when I come back here to visit."

Nicholas was stunned. "Then you and me, buddy, are very similar. Because that's exactly how I look at it. I went out there determined to make a mark. To make more money than I could ever spend, and to show my parents who tossed me away that I could be more than they ever expected. But I got no real satisfaction out of it and like you, my only real, deep joy came when I would come back here for our reunions. And so I decided that all that effort to make all that money had to have a reason.

"You know, God has a plan for us—the step that we take can all be turned for good, can all have a reason, even if we make the wrong step. Not saying that what I made was the wrong step. I probably, as you probably were, was not ready for the step we're about to take, so your words make me feel even more confident that we're on the same track. And, Wes, we're going to do good. We're going to make a difference." His brows dipped as his thoughts deepened. "We're going to take the people who need to learn the gift that riding on horseback can give them."

"Now you're talkin'." Wes nodded, his expression serious.

"They may not be able to ride by themselves," Nicholas continued. "They might even need a mechanism to help them, but I can guarantee them that whatever they need is going to be here at my ranch. And I believe that *you*, Wes, are the right man to help me make that a reality."

And the sparkle that appeared in his young, tough brother's eyes told him he was right.

# CHAPTER SEVEN

"Howdy." Edwina grinned down at Emmy and Rainy when she came to take their orders. "I'm Edwina, and I believe you must be Emmy's sister. I see a resemblance, especially in those eyes."

Rainy's brows dipped as she looked up at Edwina. "Our eyes are not the same color."

"Gotcha." Edwina grinned. "I was wondering if you were going to get my joke. You two got totally opposite eye colors but that don't mean you're not kin. What I see in those eyes is a string that goes from her eyes to your eyes. It's an attachment."

Emmy's heart squeezed tight. This woman had a way, and she saw the truth. At least her eyes had those strings on them, but as her sister met her gaze, she almost smiled.

"Yeah, I see that string too. And I've been waiting a long time to make that string shorter and get back here to my sister."

Emmy's heart throbbed hard at those words. Before she could say anything, Edwina popped her hand on her hip and studied them. "Well, girls, all I've got to say is welcome to Dew Drop. Yeah, I know you've been here a year, Emmy, but now I see a story about to unfold. You two are going to make this your home, kind of like I did. I was out there, and I found Dew Drop just like so many people do, and it changed my life for good. So you need me, you let me know. Right now, you two, you just tell me what you want and I'll run back there and tell T-bone to fix it up."

Her sister's eyes lit up. "T-bone must be a good cook because there's a lot of food on this menu—what's your favorite?"

Edwina grinned big. "Oh, well, personally, I like the chicken salad on a croissant sandwich—it's kind of elegant, you know, and good for lunch and not something I've ever eaten before coming here. I like the croissant and I have to tell you that Miss Jo, with her baking abilities, makes them fresh, just like her cakes and pies every day. And T-bone…well, just 'cause his name's T-bone doesn't mean he can't cook chicken salad. It's not something the men order very much. Well, anyway, you wanted to know, so now you know."

"Then that's what I'll have. I can't wait."

Emmy could barely speak. "I'll take the same."

Edwina looked straight at her and with the right eye, which her sister wouldn't be able to see because Edwina's head was turned slightly, she winked at Emmy, and then she turned and walked away. Edwina…the woman had a way about her.

"I like her," Rainy said, echoing Emmy's thoughts. "I have a feeling that nobody puts anything past her." She looked at Emmy hard. "And that's the way I'm going to be. Nobody, *never*, *ever* is going to put anything past me. I might be on this stinking walker and I might look weak, but I'm going to get strong. I kind of let my spirits go down at the other house. I was so ready to be my own boss. But Emmy, I'm here with you now and moments ago, I wasn't sure about anything. But now, after looking at the eyes of that lady, there's something there, like in mine, and I have a feeling she went through a lot and nothing is ever going to hurt her again." Her lips trembled as her eyes dug deep. "So, I'm thinking that maybe that man over there and his idea might help. Putting me on the back of a horse could help me with my balance. Because that's part of my problem…when I let go of these handlebars, my world kind of spins and my left side gets weak. But maybe a horse and learning to ride could help me. Can we ask him?"

Emmy's heart cinched tight with hope. "Yes. We'll let them eat but when the time is right, maybe tomorrow or if they stop by the table before they leave maybe then. Because he did offer, and you will be their first on the ranch. Their first person to help, so you have to understand that there might be some learning in that for them too."

"I'm ready. And they both look mighty strong. I think they can keep me from falling off that horse if I went to topple off. But if you'll get me some weights, I'll start working out too, from my chair. And if I had some of those bars that I could stand up in between and practice being stable, that would help too. I gave up, you know. But not anymore."

Emmy almost burst into tears. There was hope in this room, in her heart, and there was thankfulness for the man behind her who she was certain could help her sister.

\* \* \*

They ate as they talked but when they had finished, Edwina brought them their bill and he paid.

Then Wes looked at him. "Okay, so I've been watching, and they're getting up to head out, so you ready?"

Nicholas smiled at him. "I'm ready. I was hoping you were watching. Our first agenda is making sure she makes it down that track we set up for her. And I think that you might keep it in the back of your vehicle. We might even come to town and build one at the end of the sidewalk or somewhere, probably right here in front of the diner. I'm sure they'd be happy for us to do that—

Miss Jo, I mean."

"You betcha. We'll talk to her and get it done. But if your plan is like mine, she's not going to be using that walker too much longer. But since I'm new to this, I don't have a clue...that's just my hope."

They stood and headed toward the door as Emmy and Rainy headed toward it. Nicholas pushed the door open, and Wes tipped his hat at the two ladies, and then walked out the door and stood beside the rail.

"Thank you two," Emmy said as she let her sister go out the door.

Rainy looked up at him. "Thank you. It's kind of hard to open a door when your hands are on these two bars here."

"I'd open it for you no matter how or where your hands were, but I understand."

He was startled as she went out, and he saw Emmy studying him with eyes that said something had changed. She walked past him and then, when they got outside, instead of going down the plank, Rainy stopped in front of Wes, and Emmy did too. Emmy looked at him.

"So Rainy wants to take you up on your offer. And

I'm thrilled that she's very eager and determined to get better. She's even told me to get her one of those railings, you know, that have the two bars where she can let go of that thing in front of her and start working on her strength by walking in between the bars."

"I can build that for you." Wes grinned. "You just tell me when and where, and I'll put it up. Matter of fact, Nicholas, are we going to have one of those at the ranch, too? I can build both of them. Remember I told you about the guy at the rodeo whose sister was—" His gaze went to Rainy, a little stunned that he had overtalked maybe. "So you know, I'm a bull rider. And I know a bull rider whose sister is kind of in the same situation as you. And she came to a few of his rodeos. She's engaged and getting married to another rodeo cowboy, and so she came some. And, well, outside her trailer, they had one of those. And I'd see her out there working on her walking ability. Her strength training, she called it. She wanted to walk down the aisle without holding onto her walker. And I'm hoping she does 'cause she looked determined, but I can tell you her fiancé—he'd of carried her down that aisle. He loved her with all his heart just as she was; he'd take her how he could get her, but she's determined."

"I'm not getting married, I can tell you that for sure, but I'm determined to walk again. I don't know, with my hip I might limp...the limp might always be there, but I'm going to work my hardest to walk."

Wes grinned. "Then I think it's time for you to become a cowgirl. We're going to look forward to you coming out there to work with us, maybe teach us a thing or two."

Nicholas met Emmy's eyes, and he couldn't help it; he smiled. "I think we're all in. We're going to let this adventure begin, so let us get back to the ranch and get things ordered and prepared. I figure it will be a few days to get in all the saddles we might need and equipment—not that I'm thinking we're going to need that much for you, Rainy. I think we'll get you up in that saddle and you working on your stomach muscles and your thighs. We're going to work on your steadiness but we're going to be right by your side.

"Okay, so I'll tell you what...we're going to build you one of those railings. Wherever you want—you want it in your bedroom, out in your yard? We're going to put ours probably near the horse arena under that awning there. We're probably going to have a lot of things out there to help build strength and steadiness, so right there you already helped us."

"Well, there's a large back porch on the little house that I'm renting…well, that I'm buying. And I think that might be a good spot. It would be out of the rain, and it's got a smooth wooden floor. What do you think?" She looked at her sister.

"Sounds good to me. Needs to be where I can get to it every day because I guess when I'm not on a horse ride or coming to town to eat at this wonderful diner, that's where I'll be."

Wes waved at the ramp. "Then let's get you down this ramp. You two can head home, and me and my boss there, we'll get it started."

Nicholas grinned at Emmy. "Well, boss man agrees…we're going to get this party on the go."

And so, they were.

* * *

The next couple of days, Emmy and Rainy spent at the house, getting her all moved in and settled. Getting a routine set up and just spending time on the porch drinking tea, coffee, and sometimes hot cocoa with marshmallows. Getting to know each other after so long of not being around each other but on weekends was the most wonderful moments Emmy had had in her life since the day they told her that her sister was going to live.

She'd gone into a private courtyard at the hospital after the doctor had given her that news. Still unable to see her, she'd gone out there and cried her heart out in relief. Then she was able to take in the fact that the police had not charged her for the death of her heartless father—which her mother was accusing her of initating. Thankfully, the police ignored her and taken the alcoholic away. Taking up for him instead of her children had been horrible, but had been what they needed. *He* had been armed and dangerous with his truck, and after he climbed out of the truck with a metal tire tool and stormed at her, she'd defended herself. The pistol lying on the ground between them had been his condemning. After he'd fallen face first into the dirt and she'd rushed to her sister...only then he'd crawled toward the gun that lay between them.

One glance into Rainy's eyes staring up at her full of pain and Emmy didn't hesitate—she dove for the pistol. The instant it was in her grasp she aimed and she'd pulled the trigger.

He was dead.

She would live with that day for the rest of her— how she hated what she'd done, but had to do.

But now, looking at her sister, she knew she would have done it again if needed. Everything fell into place. Her life was never going to be disrupted again by some mean, hate-driven person. It was just the two of them and the past they would deal with was what they created from here on in. They'd spent two days alone, looking toward the future instead of the past, and now they were both smiling.

They were both determined that if God was willing, Rainy would walk again. Both of them had gratitude in their hearts for each other.

Rainy teared up when she thanked her for all the time she'd taken to visit with her and then to keep her safe. She thanked her for stepping in when she shouldn't have and told her bluntly to never, ever do that again.

Then they'd clasped hands and sworn that if they ever married, and it was a big capital *IF* they married, they'd make sure that the men they each married was a strong, Godly man. A man who loved with all his heart.

Emmy made the deal but wasn't thinking of herself. It was her hope, her dream that sweet Rainy would one day know true love.

Emmy had seen it walking around this town with the couples who'd found each other. There was no rush, but she'd seen love and here in Dew Drop, it was embraced. In her heart, she knew this was the place that her sister's bright future would become illuminated with the beauty she deserved.

The third morning, they were sitting out on the porch. Each of them had their drink: she had a cup of hot coffee with a touch of cream, and Rainy had a glass of orange juice today. They were thrilled when the big black four-wheel drive truck pulled into the drive. And there sat Nicholas—Nick, she had started calling him in her brain. Didn't mean anything personal; it was just shorter to think of and it fit him. Nick was down-to-earth, on target, and determined, but on top of that, he was Santa Claus, because he had the gift of giving and was determined to not only brighten their day and future but others' too, and she could do nothing but admire him for that. And thank God for sending him into their lives. Not for herself but for her sister.

Beside him and out of the truck before Nick was broad, strong Wes. The cowboy yelled hello, waved, and headed to the back end of the truck. He lowered the tailgate just as Nick walked up to the patio, and she stood.

"Good morning. You two look like you're on a mission."

He grinned, tipped his hat at her sister, and then yanked his head toward the raging bull who was now carrying a whole load of wood across the yard toward them. "Well, we've got things started up at the place. Things will be arriving supposedly this afternoon. We put a rush on everything, figured out where we wanted stuff, and we're ready to go. Horses, the best horses there are, have been delivered by Sunrise Ranch. They've been tagged by all the boys on what they thought was the best, and they can't wait to come and see how you ride one day—if that's okay with you."

"Sure."

"Great. I think you're going to like them. They range from B.J., who is nine, and Sammy, who is almost ten, to the older boys from fourteen to seventeen. And the ones who are now in college. But you'll meet them all this coming weekend at the gathering. The three oldest are Tony, Micah, and Jake. Then Caleb, who's about thirteen. That kid likes to fiddle with things, come up with ideas and build them. As long as he's been on the ranch, he's been tearing things apart and rebuilding them—sometimes parts are left off and sometimes parts are added, depending on what he's trying to achieve. Sometimes it's really cool. We all communicate, and everyone is always interested in what Caleb is working on. I'm not real sure but he's working on things to help people, so maybe this endeavor could possibly end up being a path to his destiny."

"Really?" Emmy asked, intrigued.

"We've always thought something great was going to come out of that wildly inquisitive, inventive mind of his."

He grinned, and Emmy told herself that her heart was going on a rampage in her chest because of the excitement of what he was saying about this kid—not because the man had a smile that was a deep diver into her very hard-core heart. Deep down, she was lying to herself.

This cowboy had one amazing smile, and something about it and those eyes of his gave her hope and delight…not that she was going to completely admit that or give in to it. Yes, the last three nights, lying in bed when everything was quiet, she thought of him and all he was going to do for her sister. And his smile, and those twinkling eyes full of optimism and determination came to her in the darkness giving her hope and making it very hard to shuffle away before she went to sleep.

"I think it's a great idea," Emmy said, drawing her gaze to meet Rainy's. She caught the funny look in her eyes as she studied Emmy.

Obviously, she had seen something in Emmy's eyes. Now, Emmy couldn't look back at Nick because she hoped he hadn't seen something in her eyes.

"Yes, I'm excited, about Caleb," she said. "Talking about him just filled me with the thought that we could in some way inspire him to find his path."

*Okay, maybe that helped.* Maybe, just maybe

talking about the boy she had glimpsed but never fully met could be another plus to having her sister here.

"Well, we're going to be working on it, and Rainy…" Wes said, taking over the conversation.

*Thank goodness.*

"What we're going to need is your input as we are developing things to help the others who are going to come after you."

Rainy's eyes lit up. "Really?"

"Do you think that perky mind you have and that absolute determination of yours to get better, stronger, could become part of our development process? Or as me and the guys are now calling it, our conspiracy theory to make life better for those who have been injured or are not as blessed as those of us who can get around easy."

Emmy just gaped at this boy—no, this *man*. And then she looked at her sister and Emmy saw the smile spreading across Rainy's face. Throwing her arms around Wes was her first instinct, because not only had he just given her sister another reason to walk—he had given her a mission.

# CHAPTER EIGHT

Tears swelled inside Emmy because she knew that her mission to help her sister had gotten her through hard times, and now her sister had a mission to help others too.

"Well then." Nick put his hands on his hips—his lean hips and long legs and scuffed boots that said he was ready to work.

She yanked her gaze back up to his eyes that, thank goodness, weren't looking at her but at her sister, as he continued, "We're on a mission and the first one is we're about to build *your* athletic railings. You, determined sweet young lady, are about to have a place to build those muscles. And in doing so, you can help us tweak this thing as we go."

"Seriously?" Rainy said.

"Yes. We can also order them already built, but right now we want to make sure it's exactly the size you need, so we're building it. So, let's do this."

"Yeah, let's do this." Wes grinned, and Rainy's smile radiated as the two stared at each other.

Emmy nearly cried for happiness as Rainy lifted her hand in the air and waited for Wes to give her a high five. He did, knowing exactly what her hand lifted up in the air toward him meant.

And in that moment, Emmy's gaze locked with 'Nick's and there was a bond building between all of them...not just to help her sister, but to help others.

* * *

Nicholas knew by the end of the afternoon that Wes was meant to be with him here on his ranch, helping those in need. He'd been amazing, building the bars that would enable Rainy to walk as her strength allowed her. And with each time she did work the bars, her strength would grow. Her drive would be her friend.

The young cowboy had a drive inside him, too, and Nicholas could see that he was as determined as he was to see Rainy walking. What was even better was to see the way that Rainy and Wes connected. It wasn't, as far as he could tell, an attraction but instead a purpose. It was as if the two were now driven to prove to the world that she could walk again.

And that was combined with the pure excitement the boys at the ranch had shown about getting involved. It added even more to why he was here.

As they loaded up at the end of the build and told the ladies they'd see them tomorrow at the ranch and in town for the reunion the next day, his thoughts went to the boys as they drove away.

When this dream slammed into him, he'd never thought that the guys at the ranch would want to participate like they were doing. All of them were aiming to help in some way, but there were two whose eyes had glowed strong with determination.

The first had been Tony, their very own Elvis look-alike. He was about eighteen now and had been through more terrible treatment than any boy who'd ever come through the ranch. At least as far as any of them knew, Tony's injuries were in his mind and memory, but also all over his scarred body. As scarred as he was, Tony had a destiny to help others.

Then, there was Caleb, who he felt pretty sure was destined to invent something for them.

Those boys had been through terrible things and were looking for a way to give back. This made Nicholas thankful that he might just have found a way for them to do exactly that. And that pleased him, as much as the pleasure he'd seen glowing in beautiful Emmy's eyes as she'd watched her sister helping with the new strength bars.

When Rainy grabbed the metal bars and then used her own strength to lift herself to a standing position between the two bars, he'd seen the tears glowing in Emmy's eyes. And that, as much as he was trying not to get infatuated with watching the woman, had affected him.

It had enforced his want, his need to make this difference in her sister's life and the lives of others. Including his brothers from the Sunrise Ranch.

He smiled, driving toward the sun that was starting to lower at the end of the straight country road. But instead of thinking about the sunset, he was thinking about the saying at the ranch, the Sunrise Ranch, where the sun rose every day with their determination to let it shine.

He saw that today and knew that tomorrow when Rainy came to ride a horse, he would see it more.

He would also see Emmy, and he couldn't help but think about that, too.

* * *

*It was a beautiful morning in so many ways*, thought Emmy, the day after the rails had been built on her back porch. They were headed to Nick's ranch, where her sister was going to ride a horse for the first time. Tomorrow, they would go to town for the reunion. Rainy's first week in town was full, and that pleased them both.

"I'm really excited about this," Rainy said as they drove into the tall iron entrance to Nick's ranch. "Today,

I ride a horse. And then fun tomorrow in town and Wes told me there would be fishing at the Sunrise Ranch on Sunday afternoon."

"It does all sound great."

"Of course, I know I'll just watch the fishing. But today I get to ride."

"I'm so excited you'll get to ride. But I have to tell you that Drewbaker and Chili are going to fish on Sunday, and I think they are bringing their special fishing trough."

"A what?"

Emmy grinned. "Everyone talks about a few years ago when they brought a big round water trough like the ones cows drink water out of, or some people use for small swimming pools. Anyway, these two use it as a joke to put in the water and fish from. I was told Wes helped them get it into the lake last time and is going to help again."

"That would be fun to see."

"Then we will get there early enough on Sunday to watch it happen. It will be fun."

"And today will be too," Rainy said as Emmy

pulled to a halt in front of the large metal barn, from which Wes and Nick were going to change her sister's life. She was excited about today—*for that reason and that reason alone.*

The late-afternoon sunlight glistened on the metal. She had had to work today. Thankfully, she'd hired part-time help who had worked in her place. And she would do that on Saturday as well.

Emmy was blessed that she could even afford part-time help. If at all possible, she was going to work on getting an online store opened too. But right now, she was going to watch her sister ride a horse.

"Oh, my goodness…look! That horse is beautiful," Rainy said, excitement in her voice.

From the SUV parked in front of the arena where Nick had told her to park, they saw, tied to the fence, a beautiful golden horse. And on its back was a special saddle that had a back attached for support and straps she assumed were for Rainy's legs. None of them knew how sturdy her sister would be, but she smiled as she looked at the saddle. Nick had thought of everything. As she turned the motor off, the man strode from the barn, leading a horse. And Wes followed, leading yet another horse.

They were beauties...*the horses,* she reminded herself when her gaze settled on Nick upon thinking those words.

He was, too, but she didn't let her mind linger there.

The horse Nick led was smaller and had a regular saddle on it and looked far too small than he would ride. Wes was going to ride the large horse, although, to be honest, it was made smaller by the size of the broad-shouldered cowboy. She got out and before she'd gotten around to get the walker out for her sister, Nick had already done it and her sister hadn't hesitated in the door. She stood, gripping the edges of the doorframe as he set the walker in front of her.

"Good morning, ladies. I hope y'all are as excited as we are." Nick grinned.

Wes laughed. "I am so ready for this. And this here is the horse your sister will ride. We decided you weren't the only one who needed the fun of riding in her life. That way, we can all enjoy time out on the open fields."

Shock ricocheted through Emmy, and the grin that blew up on Rainy's face at the words made the excitement even more powerful. She could hardly speak as she looked at the pretty two-toned horse with big brown eyes, a white streak down its nose, and a golden spot on its forehead that moved between his ears and then down the side of his neck and splayed out on his side. The mingled tones were like her mind at the moment, rolling around in excitement. This was a very artistic-looking horse. *And it was for her?*

Her gaze went to Nick and his lips hitched up as he said, "This is the horse you'll ride, if you want to. He's gentle, and the boys love him. His name is Golden Mingle. I'm not sure exactly where it came from but as you can see, his golden hair mingles with everything else." He chuckled and she did, too, because it was true. "We're not riding today, only Rainy, but I wanted to show you and invite you to join the riding on the other days.'

She reached out and ran her hand along the horse's neck. "It's perfect. And I love the idea of riding too."

"Good."

Wes ran a hand along Golden Mingle's side. "When the horses are born, the fellas name them. We have a lot of funny-named horses on the ranch. And, well, this one was christened as the one for you."

"They trust its ability," Nick added. "And I know that you'll be able to ride her while your sister is riding her well-trained, calm horse with its enhanced saddle." He smiled at Rainy, and she chuckled.

"I'm excited to ride in the enhanced saddle." Her eyes danced, and they all grinned at her.

"Great," Nick said. "This horse is tame, easygoing, and has a smooth walk that they are sure will ease you into the saddle. I have ridden her, and the boys are right in what they thought in suggesting these two rides. So, what do you say, Rainy—are you ready to ride today to get you ready for a longer ride?"

"Yes," Rainy said instantly. "You two cowboys just tell me how I'm going to get up there and ride."

Emmy loved the excitement in her sister's words and her face. "I think it's a brilliant idea to get her ready and then to get me on one too. I've never ridden a horse, but I'm excited about it." She smiled at Nick. "I thought

I was just going to have to watch my sister do this but the very idea that I can go along thrills me, Nick." It hit her in that moment that she actually called him Nick. She almost gasped but caught it as she saw the look in his eyes.

That look told her that he had caught the word, and there was a softening in the cinnamon-toned eyes that did something inside her. "And, Wes, thank you, too. Y'all are going to make a difference in our lives and so many others."

"We're planning on it," Wes said, as Nick walked over to her sister.

Thank goodness, because it meant he wasn't looking at her any longer and she could breathe once more. But she caught Wes grinning at her. And then he winked before he walked over to her sister too. The horse followed him.

Emmy couldn't move; she just stood there, totally sidetracked by what was going through her. She had loved…absolutely loved the look that had come into Nicholas's eyes when she had called him Nick.

# CHAPTER NINE

*Nick.* She'd called him Nick, and he'd liked it. He had been trying to focus on this dream of his lately but every time he saw her, he had to refocus on his dream and not on that amazing love that sparked from her when she looked at her sister.

Yet, he also knew by the look on her face that she had been as shocked as he was that she'd called him a nickname. So, he had refocused on his mission on getting Rainy on the back of a horse. And he needed to.

Rainy started rolling her walker toward her horse. Her limp, her left hip swaying out, and the pressure of her hands on the walker were hard on her, evident in the strain he saw in the tops of her hand and grip as she was determined to get to her horse quick as she could. When she was that anxious, her limp was more obvious because her stride was longer, and he thought she also hurt. But she obviously didn't care. She was one determined young lady.

"What's my horse's name?"

"Dreammaker."

"This horse has been with us awhile and was actually Wes's horse."

Both Emmy's and Rainy's gazes locked onto Wes.

"Yep, this beauty I have all the confidence in the world in. I rode her the last several years I was on the ranch. So, I can tell you this horse knows how to behave, knows how to walk smoothly, and has heart. I trained her, and she helped me on many rides that I needed to be calmed down and soothed when…" He paused, as if realizing he'd said more than he wanted to.

Then he dipped his chin, looked back up, and continued, "Times when I needed to calm down from anger that built, well, sometimes still builds inside me from my crazy past. But I can tell you that's why I know horses are good, and this is going to be a success. And you, Rainy, are going to get to ride my horse. Tony, my buddy, took him after I left, Tony got great use out of him too. You're going to like Tony, he's your age, and well, everyone knows that Tony has lived through more *crud* than any of us. But that kid—*no*," he grinned. "That *man* looks like Elvis—doesn't sing like Elvis—but he has heart. He might not be able to give you a song but he's a giver. He'll give anything he's got to someone if they need it. Me included. He taught me to fight—not with my fist but with my emotions. With my mind."

That was why Wes was meant to be back in this town. That cowboy was meant to help others. And by the expressions on the sisters faces Wes had made his mark on them too.

Emmy was stunned by the strong cowboy's words and watched as his gaze locked on her sister. Emmy's gaze shot to Nicholas and she saw the certainty shinning in his proud eyes as he saw what she saw. This bull rider, this tough, strong bullrider had a heart—that glowed with care as he talked to her sister.

"My little brother, Tony taught me to push myself

and to let go. Yeah, I don't do it as good as him. As much as he's been through, he's a real giver. Anyway, you'll meet him and you'll see what I'm saying but this sweet gal right here is his gift to you. Even though he doesn't know you, he said to give you his horse, and she would be your feet. She would be your *strength*. And she will help *you* make your dreams come true. And I agree completely, because I had ridden her so long, here she is.

"Nickolas you want to butt in?"

Nick grinned. "Nope, you've got this."

"Okay, so, now, me and my *big* brother are going to have to lift you up today. We'll be careful. We're not sure how you take being lifted but we've got special contraptions coming. So I'm kind of stepping on Nicholas's toes here by telling you all this instead of letting him do it. Are you okay with us helping you do that?"

He gave Nick credit where it was probably due, the cowboy had class. She watched her sister grin, and that warmed Emmy's heart.

Rainy hitched a hand in the air, "Hey, you two, I

have been lifted, moved and even tossed around ever since this happened when I was eight. So, I'm used to being moved around by other people. But...the difference is you two are going to help me and officially be the *last* two who help me because *we*—together and with all those others from the ranch, including Tony, who I can't wait to meet—*we* are going to get this figured out. Then we can help others. If you don't mind me helping." Her gaze locked Nick then Wes, and Emmy's heart clinced tight as both cowboys grinned together, clearly loving her determination.

As did Emmy.

\* \* \*

Nick was relieved that it hadn't been hard getting Rainy into the saddle. Yes, he could tell that it hurt her some, but she said her hip hurt most of the time so she ignore it, and everyone else should too.

She had determination that was for sure.

Wes was just as determined as he carried her up the ramp then eased her into the saddle. "You're going to do good."

"Thanks, that's my plan," Rainy said, looking pretty stable.

Nick made sure and held the horse steady. "So how does that feel, that back part? Is it giving you support?" Nick asked then he took a strap attached to the special saddle and and wrapped it across the leg near him. While Wes would be strapping the other leg, he kept his hands on her shoulders until she told them all was good.

"It feels good," Rainy said. "I get it, because yes, there is the possibility that if I'm not steady enough without the back I would topple off the horse. So, like you two guessed, I wouldn't want to do that. Falling off might injure me more and that is not an option I'm good with. So good job, you two. Now," she beamed at Wes, "you can let go of my shoulder and strap that other leg in place, then teach me how to guide this horse wherever we're going."

Wes did exactly as she said, strapping the top of her leg into the top strap. They both asked how it felt and when she said it was fine, they both moved to the strap on her lower leg.

Her grinning sister watched, and so did Rainy.

*This is amazing*, Nick thought.

Wes took the reins. "I'm going to lead you slowly, and you tell me how it feels. Today we aren't going anywhere but on this level ground in a circle. You're going to let us know how stable you feel."

"Yes, we need to know if we need to adjust anything," Nick added. "You have to tell us because we need you secure in the seat. And then we go from there."

"I can do that. Right now, I feel secure. I have my hands on this saddle horn but I want my hands holding the reins, but I trust that big ole strong cowboy there to get me there. So, let's do this."

Wes grinned then started to walk, leading the horse into the area with Rainy smiling.

\* \* \*

Unable to help herself, Emmy walked over, and, to her disbelief, she threw her arms around Nick before she knew what was happening, placed her head against his shoulder and squeezed him tightly. "Thank you. This is the miracle I've been praying for." Her voice trembled, and she knew she'd stunned him as much as she'd stunned herself.

His hands remained at his side and it hit her what she'd done. She stiffened and started to pull away but then his arms came around her, and he hugged her back.

"Believe me, we are going to give this everything we've got. I feel that your sister is going to be all right."

She leaned back and met his smile. Her heart thundered rapidly at his words and the feel of being in his arms. It was a feeling she had never dreamed about. A feeling she'd never let herself think about. All she'd ever thought about was getting her sister home. And in that moment, she stepped back.

"Thank you. Thank you very much. I trust you."

And then she walked to the arena and placed her elbows on the railing that was even with her shoulders, leaned in, and watched her sister, whose back, thank goodness, was still facing away from her as Wes led her around the large round pen. She watched her sister ride and restated the reason she was doing this: her life and all she did was for Rainy.

Feeling her heart swell with what she'd just felt in Nick's arms was not part of the plan.

"I love it," Rainy called as they had made the first circle around the round pen.

Wes had led her carefully and was grinning, too. "I remember the first time I got on a horse after I was given the gift of moving to Sunrise Ranch. It was a thrill and, as you can see, I never backed down from it. To me now, riding a horse is where I feel great. I love it. I don't take my anger out on the back of a horse. I don't ride like a maniac across the fields in danger of holes that different critters dig. No, that's where my bull riding came in."

Emmy watched as he looked over his shoulder at her sister, who was taking in his words. Emmy was too.

She was glad his words carried across the pen to her as he began again. "We never met our mom, Lydia, because she died before her dream became a reality. But because of her dream, so many of us grew up over there on that large ranch across the road. Our father,

Randolph, who we all call our dad, he had had an accident on a bull. We've never been told that, but it's what we suspect happened because the one thing we aren't allowed to do on the ranch is ride a bull. And not that I went against much at the ranch...I couldn't help it."

He looked at her and then Nick, who now stood beside her. "I'll just be honest with y'all. I figure if I'm going to help anyone who needs it, then I have to be upfront. So, the anger in me was so deep from my past that a bull drew me. A wild bull—a raging bull. And when I could ride one, I got the satisfaction that I had overcome. But, I had to do it in respect for the man I love, Randolph McDermott. I did it off the ranch." He looked at Nick again.

Emmy did, too, and saw that this admission was no surprise to Nick.

"Yeah, I'm pretty positive that all the smart dudes who raised me knew I was doing that. When I went to college and instantly got accepted to the rodeo team and started winning competitions, y'all weren't surprised at all. Though, what surprised me was how happy everyone was for me."

"Yes, we were," Nick said.

Wes looked from him back to Rainy. "We do what we need to do to overcome and well, I just want you to tell me if there is anything I can do. Because I know this is where I'm supposed to be. I searched all my life, but I can tell you, Rainy Swanson, seeing you up there riding this horse and knowing that you're going to be holding these reins soon, and me riding beside you rather than walking beside you—it makes my day. So, just letting you know. And you two standing over at the fence, we're going to do this."

*Oh goodness, this was going to be wonderful.* She looked up at Nick then yanked her gaze away to focus on Wes. "I believe you now see your destiny and with that young man giving his testimony like that. This is meant to be. It's another reason I was led here to Dew Drop, the town of miracles waiting to happen."

As she said the words Wes grinned at Rainy as he led her away from them in the round pen. She looked at

Nick.

He was waiting, his gaze on her. "And that's why I came back. I have a drive inside of me. I thought it was to prove something to my parents but no, it's to share that determination with others, and I found a cohort in Wes. Everyone knew that something drives him inside. He never talks about it. He gave so much to everyone; he's a giver. I don't know that we'll ever know what all he went through but I do know this is where he is meant to be. And in all honesty, I see that drive in your sister's eyes. When we get her to walking, however a manner God's will is for her, then she's welcome here if she wants to help and be an inspiration to others. My prayer is she's going to be a walking miracle."

Tears filled her eyes and she wanted to hug him again. Holding back with everything in her, she nodded, then turned her attention back to her sister, moving with the rhythm of the horse as they circled the arena once more.

*Life goes on.*

Yes, she was here to testify to that. There had been

moments all those years ago when she'd thought all was lost. But now, she saw that there was and always had been a legacy. In all of their lives, as she looked at Rainy, Wes, and then back at Nick, she saw the reasons. Life for them now was moving on and in all their futures, she saw hope and a reason for their hardships…they could help others despite where they'd been. What mattered now was where they were going.

Sucking back the tears, she looked at Nick and smiled with all of her heart—for what he was doing for her sister. And only that.

# CHAPTER TEN

Nana McDermott, Miss Jo, and Mabel Tilsbee had a booth set up outside of the Spotted Cow Café, surrounded by all the pots of red geraniums on the wide patio. To her surprise, leading up to the patio and not needed right now, was a new wheelchair ramp that had been built and now there was a parking space beside it, making it all official. Dew Drop now had a place where someone in a wheelchair, or someone like her could move with a walker to the sidewalk much easier. The sight made her heart swell, but also the thought that her sister might not have to use it. Still, it was good to have for anyone coming to this tiny town to access. If her sister did have to use it, this was a wonderful gift.

"Let's do this." Rainy grinned up at her as she

pushed her walker and they headed down the main road that had been blocked off for the day. "Those three ladies are looking like they are ready to hand out something really great to eat and drink."

"You and I both know if Miss Jo is there, they have all kinds of pie and probably coffee, lemonade—something good to go with the pies."

They reached them, and Miss Jo walked straight to Rainy and hugged her. "We want you to know that we have an official chair here for you to use when you're tired and want to sit down. You don't have to, but we are going to have fun handing out food everyone will love. This is going to be a great day. If you want to go see people racing in the three-legged races or throwing cow patties in competition, then you can sure do it. And we have a whole slew of young cowboys who have offered to watch over you. Don't let that make you angry. Believe me, every one of them have been watched over at some point in time since they came to our town. And of course, Edwina is inside taking care of business, for anyone who wants more than the pies, coffee, and lemonade we have out here, if you want some of that or want to sit inside."

She'd been right in what they were offering here at the booth to eat and drink. Emmy loved this town.

Rainy's gaze had crossed the street to the group of boys now, she looked back at Miss Jo. "That chair is going to come in handy at some point, so thank y'all. But that group of fellas over there…I'm looking to meet them."

Emmy smiled, looked at the wide-smiling Nana. "Wave them over so they can stop standing there waiting. I want to meet them too."

"Great," Rainy added. "There are some in that group who have plans for the horse-riding camp and I really want to meet them."

Emmy knew she was talking specifically about Tony. Her sister had mentioned him last night. She wondered about someone who had obviously touched big, strong Wes so deeply, and she did too. And as Miss Jo waved and the boys headed their way, it wasn't hard to pick Tony out.

He didn't rush; he was tall, lean, and he looked like a young Elvis. He followed everyone. A hat on his head made his wavy black hair curl out from below. He had that face of Elvis, and even from the distance as he crossed the road, his eyes, well, even the young ones who didn't even know who Elvis was knew that this kid—young man—stood out. It wasn't just the blue eyes and handsome face; it was that expression…that Elvis expression that said he had a soft spot in his heart. And as the boys approached, Emmy couldn't help but wonder what had happened to him. It was obviously so bad that everyone seemed to realize it was terrible.

"Hey, I'm B.J. I'm the youngest kid, and it's good to meet you." The little boy grinned as he held out his hand. All the others stood back and let him talk.

Rainy took his offered hand in her right hand and held tightly to the handle with her other. "It's really good to meet you, B.J. You look like you know how to live."

"That's what they tell me. I ride a horse, and I know you're learning now so maybe you can go on a roundup with us."

"A roundup sounds fun, but after I'm steady in the saddle."

"Yeah, you don't want to fall off," the next smallest boy said, his eyes held a seriousness. "I'm Sammy and excited that you're learning to ride, too. Riding a horse helps me when I'm feeling sad. And everyone will tell you we also learned how to ride a kayak in the river. It's something that I kinda didn't do good at first but now I really enjoy it. Maybe one day after you get good on that horse and you're able to move around good, we can get you out on the water. Believe me, you'll want to make sure you're ready for that. But this is the right place for all of that."

She looked at all the boys and her gaze met Nana, who raised her eyebrow. "Yes, believe us when we say that riding in the kayak needs to come later. Mr. Sammy found that out, thank the Lord our Jolie, a professional kayaker, knew how to get him out before he drowned."

Rainy smiled at the boy. "I'm glad you survived, and you've given me another target to aim for after I get on my feet again. Smooth water kayaking, not hard rapids, but floating on calm water sounds fun. I saw a movie last year about a woman who was paralyzed after she fell off the top of a building. She was paralyzed from her mid-back down. She had the use of her arms but nothing else.

"That movie helped me as I watched it. I could have been in a much worse situation. You reminded me of that movie. I watched her dream of being able to move around free again, and she found that in a kayak. So thanks for the reminder, and one day I'm going to do that too. So, I'll get back to introductions now. Who are you?" she asked the next one in line.

Emmy loved how her sister acted and as each boy told who he was, a group of adults gathered around. Emmy knew they were the original McDermott men and their wives. They stood back and watched as each boy introduced themselves. There were sixteen boys and she couldn't remember all of them but she would work at remembering each one. Then there was Caleb; he was blond and thin.

"So you're Caleb," Rainy said. "I'm excited to work with you. You sound like you have good ideas. When they told me you're inquisitive and always looking at things, trying to make it better, it got my brain to working. If I think I could use something, maybe you could invent—is that what it would be called?"

Caleb grinned hugely. "Th-that's kind of what I call it." He stuttered a little bit. "All the fellas like to come look at the stuff in the part of the barn where I work. But I have to warn you that sometimes I don't know what I'm working on or coming up with. I just see something, and I dig in."

Her sister's eyes lit up more. "That sounds cool. Maybe I'll see if I can come out and see it all. Um, when my sister gets off work, maybe she can bring me out."

That's when Tony stepped up. "Hi, I'm Tony."

Rainy straightened as much as possible, forcing more weight on her elbows as she did so. "I thought you were. It's nice to meet you, and thank you for my horse. He's wonderful. You and Wes trained him well."

Tony smiled that crooked Elvis Presley smile.

*Goodness gracious.* Emmy was stunned watching him—and her sister's actions too.

Then he tipped his hat. "On the driving subject, if your sister agrees—I'd be more than happy to come pick you up and take you to the ranch. You could hang out with us some. We'd take care of you—I mean, make sure you're safe. I have to tell you that Caleb's brain works. He's got some cool things over there, and we all enjoy testing them out. Not sure you could do that with some of them, but some you could." He paused and met Emmy's gaze with his Elvis eyes. "She'd enjoy it, ma'am. And I can promise you she'd be safe."

Emmy didn't hesitate. "Tony, I believe you. I think everything I heard is that you guys are amazing. No one has said anything about you that wasn't positive. So, if she wants you to pick her up, have an adventure seeing what y'all do, then yes, I agree, but that's up to her. After all, she is seventeen."

That got a grin from Rainy. "You bet I am. I'm a determined seventeen, and Tony, we're going to do this. Thanks to all of y'all. So I hear that I have escorts all day, so let's go. Let's move it on out. Lead the way and show me what's good to eat, what's fun to watch, and where I can sit down and rest every once in a while. Miss Jo, Miss Mabel, and Nana have me this great seat. But I have a feeling once we get down the road, seeing all these booths and then all the adventures y'all are telling me about, I'll need another spot to rest my tensed-up back."

Wes stepped up, grinning, and on his back, he had one of those chairs that folds up and straps on like a sling. He took it from his shoulder and passed it to the first hand that reached out for it, which was Tony's.

"Thank you, sir. We've got this. If you need to sit down, we'll open this up and make sure you have a good view of whatever you want to see, whatever is going on."

Her heart couldn't take it all in. "All of you young folks have a great time. And I'll be here, wandering around some myself but today, Rainy, this is your day. Y'all have fun."

Her sister grinned. "I plan to. Thank you."

And with that, she started to push her walker and the entire herd of cowboys began to walk beside her, timing their strides with hers. Everyone in the street parted as the group surrounding her sister made their way past them.

"That's our boys," Nana said.

Emmy looked at the beautiful older lady, with her gray hair pulled back into a ponytail, and watched the heartfelt smile spread across her face digging deep.

"You're amazing…all of you are," Emmy said, meaning it with all of her heart. "I'm so glad we're here."

\* \* \*

Nicholas stood away from everyone, watching Emmy let go of her sister by not standing in the way of her walking off with the fellas. She was giving Rainy independence. It was hugely important, and he was proud of Emmy. He could tell she was extremely protective. He didn't know the story but there was a reason for that, and he wanted to know what it was, if possible. He had a feeling he'd have to build her trust for that to happen.

"Looks like they're going to fit in well," Morgan said as he moved to stand beside him.

"Yes, they are. They're determined. I don't know what they went through but there is a connection there between her and all of them."

"You see it too. Because that's what I think too.

And, those two over there." He nodded to Chili and Drewbaker. "I believe they know something. You see how they're watching her. And now look…they're getting up. They're going to trail them to make sure she's okay."

"Not that she's going to get in trouble with the guys. They're going to take good care of her, but I agree, maybe in case she falls down or something. Those two dudes watch out for everyone."

"They're good at it." It was true. "I think opening the place was exactly what I was supposed to do. Wes fits right in, and I have a feeling Tony and Caleb may have found their place. Though, in my heart of hearts, I believe Caleb's going to build something spectacular one day and we're all going to get to say we knew he would."

Morgan nodded. "I agree. And we're all going to be rooting him on, clapping all the way. Who knows, it could be something that helps a person fly in the sky by themselves."

They laughed because they both knew he worked with all kinds of things out there in his barn area. "It'll be fun to watch. Morgan, your mom's dream has been amazing."

"Yeah, I know. And see Dad over there? That handsome, strong man leaning against that post, surrounded by all of his buddies, he and my—our awesome Nana made it all come true."

"Yep, but everyone knows that you, and your brothers with you, are going to take it to the next level. There's no telling how many fellas like me are going to walk this path. Look down there at all those who are getting here, who have grown up with us and are here to meet up. We're going to have to go meet them all and get this reunion started. I see Abe Bradshaw, who moved to Star Gazer Island. That's his bride. She's about to have a day like Emmy and Rainy, a first experience at our Sunrise Ranch and Dew Drop, Texas reunion."

Morgan grinned. "Yeah, I think so. They had a beautiful wedding on that beach. You probably saw the photos Nana shared in her letter she sends out to everyone, keeping us connected."

"I did see them. That's how I recognized them now."

"So many of our brothers move on and find great lives and love out there and that's my mom's dream come true. We'll always be having these reunions and hoping everyone comes back to visit so we stay in touch. And that crowd of young ones surrounding Rainy will get older, and we'll be watching them and their sweethearts come join us one day. Speaking of that, how about you?" Morgan turned so he was looking straight at Nicholas. "Are you ever going to fall in love and bring Nana some grandbabies to cuddle?"

Nicholas didn't mean to, but his gaze went straight to Emmy, who was now helping Nana, Miss Jo, and Mabel at their table. "I haven't really looked. That unsettled feeling inside me never lets me think about that next step. As much as I threw myself into my work, it took all my time, and my heart was cinched up tight. But, I'll admit to you, Morgan, that something about coming back here, back home, gave me a sense of contentment. I feel like I'm where I'm supposed to be and looking at you happy and all my brothers happy, I'm on the lookout."

Unable to stop it, his gaze went right back to that beautiful woman. Her arms around him yesterday had not been forgotten. He'd hugged her back and loved it, but then they'd both pretended that the hug hadn't happened. *But it had happened. Big time.*

"I think I saw that, even though I probably wasn't supposed to." Morgan studied him and grinned.

"Something about her draws me," he said, no need to deny it to Morgan. "Not just because she is beautiful, but something else. Like nothing I've ever felt before."

"Well, that's a normal feeling when you meet someone special. Someone who could be that special woman in your life. My married brothers have all felt that. All I can tell you is don't hide from it. And don't…well, I could say don't rush it, but who knows? When it happens, it happens. But remember, sometimes love takes a little grit, a little determination, and patience. But most of all it takes a heart that gives and takes."

He sighed, knowing it was all true. "Yep, but right now, my only plan is to give her what she desires, and that is to see her sister walk. And *that* is where my focus is going to be."

# CHAPTER ELEVEN

After making sure Emmy helped the ladies at the table for a while, her gaze going down the street to watch her sister enjoying herself with her escorts.

"So, you and your cute sister are going out to ride at Nicholas's place?" Nana asked, a gentle, encouraging smile on her face.

Emmy glanced and saw that Miss Jo and Mabel were just as interested in her answer. "Yes. He and Wes are helping her, and from the looks of it, all the other fellas from your ranch are in on it too. I can't tell you how thankful I am for this. There is no way to say it…I chose Dew Drop because of you ladies. When I came here, y'all welcomed me, and Nana, though I didn't meet you on my trip here that first time, you still influenced my decision. Because of how dedicated you and your son and your grandsons were to helping boys who need to know they are loved. And Rainy needed to know that, too, so I chose Dew Drop because of that."

She watched as her sister and her group had reached an area farther down, and they were watching someone get dunked and were participating in tossing balls at the target. She smiled. "I don't even know how long it's been since she smiled like that. Even from this distance, it's visible in its radiance."

"Those boys," Nana said, "are used to welcoming fellow boys to the ranch. And helping them with their troubles. Helping them get through and overcome. It's known that not all of them overcome as they need to or that we hope for them to. But they still learn to push it aside and live. And..." She glanced at the others. "And we as a group of buddies watch them and do what we can to at least help them move forward. Nicholas is one of those. He was driven from day one on the ranch. Poor kid, his parents simply kicked him out onto the street as a little boy and moved on."

Emmy hadn't been kicked out but would have left

early on her own if Rainy hadn't been born. She never regretted her sister coming into her life. She was the reason Emmy found purpose in life. Looking at Nick, she felt that was what he had been searching for and was now finding it.

She focused on Nana as she continued, "I'm fairly certain he knows where his parents are, if they're alive or dead. But even if he hadn't made his own money, our ranch would have given him money to start his new life with.

"But that driven fella paid the ranch back as soon as he made his first big check and told us to use it for others. He is a great man. A driven man. And we're glad he finally found something that is truly going to make him happy because until now he hadn't been."

Emmy's insides trembled as her gaze went across the street, and she watched him talking to his brothers. Her heart swelled, and she yanked her gaze away and back to Nana. "He's going to change my sister's life. Wes, too. I think, from what I gathered, that Wes also has demons that follow him. I have told no one but I have those demons myself. Being here helps me in more ways than any of you can know."

Miss Jo reached out and placed a hand on her arm. "I felt from day one when you came into my diner that there was something in the background of your life that drove you. You're one smart cookie…because out of all the places you could have chosen to call home, you chose Dew Drop. You chose *us*, and we're here for you. If you need to talk to someone there are a lot of us, though in your heart of hearts, you'll know the right person to talk to."

They were all looking at her with such love, and tears welled inside her. She hadn't cried in forever; she'd thrown tears out years ago. She brought her tears to her heart and punched them away anytime they threatened. Tears had no place in her life. "Thank y'all. And believe me, I have never told anyone what I just told you three. Because of the hearts that you have. So I don't know if I'll ever say anything more; I'm just grateful that I have my sister with me now. And, that…yes, my prayers were answered in that she can be free and He put me here. And that He's given her a group who can help lead her and strengthen her. I just know that she's going to be okay. And…I know if, by some craziness, I were to get sick and die, I know she's in a great place here with all of you. I can always rest easy knowing that she is in a great place."

"Now, now." Mabel strode to her and placed both her hands on her biceps. "You just *stop* talking like that. Why would you start thinking about dying when you just moved to Dew Drop and it is time to live? *Live*, my friend. You need to take all the past you have that is struggling with your heart, and you need to just throw it in the mud and stomp on it. *This* is your new beginning, and no matter what happened in your past, you have a heart of hearts. You did what you could to bring your sister a good life when she was finally able to come to you from a shelter. A shelter that was able to watch over her until you could. Now, look at me…I'm serious. I fly all over the world, helping people survive disasters. It is my dream, my goal. I have that historic, beautiful inn over there that has come from a history that dates way, way back and survived to be the beauty that it is. For instance, that inn used to be a—well, let's just say there were shenanigans that went on in there that I would never have anything to do with.

"But I've taken it and made it into what I want it to be. None of its history, bad history or even the good history, matters. None of it. What matters now is that it's in my possession and it's what I give to it that helps it be the Dew Drop Inn. A welcoming place to people who are visiting, like you. I have wonderful people who work there who I keep because they are also glad to see and meet wonderful people.

"Now, if I had let the inn's bad parts cause me to shut it down, it wouldn't be here. And part of the beauty of Dew Drop is the Dew Drop Inn, and I know it. I'm proud of the good things that come from it. Not the fact that long ago it was a...brothel. But it's not now and never will it go back to its beginning because it is the *past*. Now, dear lady, it's time for *you* to shut the door on whatever it is that causes the pain that we can see in your eyes. Shut the door—slam the door and live life from today forward. Get to know someone who you can trust and tell your heart's secrets. Secrets that need to be let out. Or, go find you a beautiful stream, find you a rock and sit on it, say a prayer and then let it go."

Her heart was raging, and she was trembling. She knew Mabel, deep-thinking Mabel, could feel her arms trembling beneath the fingers tenderly holding onto her arms. "Thank you. So, I think since I have to open my heart a bit, I'll take a walk and try to let some of this out. Just watching the fun people are having." She tried hard to keep her words even as she spoke. "I'll be back. And thank y'all."

Mabel released her and gave Emmy a smile, as did Miss Jo and Nana. She turned and headed down the street. She needed time alone.

She needed a place to…cry.

* * *

Nicholas saw the deep conversation going on between Emmy and the ladies. He also thought he saw emotion, strong emotion, as he watched Emmy and then saw her walk away. Then his gaze was met by three sets of eyes when he glanced back at the ladies, looking for a reason why the emotion had been in her face. He stared at them, and then Nana gave him a nod.

*The nod.* Nana had watched many young boys at the ranch struggle with deep trauma and emotions. She tried to get through, but she'd known when someone else needed to step in and talk. He often had done that. Tried, anyway…and he only did it with someone who was struggling and when Nana looked him straight in the eyes and gave him *the nod.* Now, without hesitation, he excused himself from talking to his brothers, and he strode down the road. There were people everywhere and when he had been looking at Nana and the ladies, 'Emmy had disappeared in the crowd.

He stopped walking and glanced around. The alley to his right led to the open fields, and there he spotted her. She'd chosen to walk away from everyone, to be alone, and he followed her.

As he approached, she moved over to the side, taking her out of view of anyone who glanced down the alley, including him if he'd glanced that way seconds too late. She raked her hand through her beautiful hair, and he saw it trembling as she pulled it from her strands and slammed it to her hip. He paused just a few feet behind her. Had to pause or he would have walked straight up to her, pulled her into his arms, and told her he would make everything right. He had no idea whether he could make it all right, but it was all he wanted to do. Whatever troubled her, whatever was deep in those eyes of hers, he knew that he'd seen in eyes before in all his years at Sunrise Ranch—the home for unloved, beaten, rejected, abused in all sorts of ways boys. He recognized when someone just needed to talk, to get it out.

"Emmy, can I help?" His words were low.

She didn't even turn. Her shoulders drooped a little more.

"I don't think—anyone can help me. I just want to do what the ladies told me and find a way to push it all away. To do that and enjoy the happy life I see with my sister."

Her voice was trembling, and so were her shoulders. Unable to stop himself because he didn't want to, he strode past her, turned to look at her, and saw the tears rolling down her cheeks. He instantly wrapped his arms around her. He buried his face in her hair. "Don't cry. Tell me what you need. Talk to me.

Believe me, Emmy, I've had to talk before, and I've also listened to many stories from boys who just needed to talk. Sometimes, you just have to talk."

There was no sound, just the trembling, and he could tell she was still crying. All he could do was hold her, smell the soothing scent of her hair that had him burying his face in it, but he was in that moment most focused on getting her to stop crying.

"I'm here for you," he said. "And I think I'm supposed to be. I know that sounds crazy, but I've felt that from the moment I first saw you. God connects people for a reason, and I feel that now. Trust me, nothing you tell me goes anywhere but between you and me."

Her arms went around him. He tried not to let the emotion of the movements thrill him, but it did. It told him that she needed him, and she trusted him. He knew she was about to tell him whatever it was that haunted her, so he waited.

Emmy leaned her head back and looked at him, her eyes full of pain. "I took abuse almost from day one from my father." Her words came out broken.

His heart hardened with fury for the abuser—*her father*. He wanted to slam the man against—he held back words as she continued speaking.

"My mother just let it happen. She never tried to help me and when I was a beaten down twelve-year-old girl, my baby sister was born. I had always been thankful that I was an only child, that no one else was in my family who had to go through what I did. But when Rainy was born, I loved her from the moment I saw her and I tried to watch out for her. But when she was about a year old he picked her up and threw her across the room. She slammed against the wall and fell to the floor."

"I'm so sorry the two of you went through that," he gritted out, furious at this—creep—other words raced through his mind as his rage roared.

"*Anger* boiled through me as I raced to get to her. I had been beaten by him, but this was different, when I saw Rainy being mistreated, wrath erupted and I hit him. He instantly hit me back, knocked me to the ground but for the first time ever, I got back up. I was so angry that I barely felt his fist and from that day forward he took his anger out on me because I'd fought back—but I wanted that instead of on my baby sister."

Fury exploded through him and his arms tightened around her as he felt her rampaging heart thunder against his. "Then what happened?" he managed, fighting to keep his voice steady.

"After that I always made sure Rainy was in other rooms when he was home. I also taught her to hide in special places, be silent and wait for me to come get her if she heard angry words. She did exactly what I asked her to do early on, but as she grew older, she saw what was happening and she started to get angry. That's when I knew I had to do something else to keep her safe."

His anger grew with each word as she continued, as if having to talk fast to get the words out.

"She was about to turn eight, and one day we came home from school, and they were both so drunk that they weaved as they were crossing the rough yard, and he shoved Rainy out of the way as they headed toward the truck. Seeing them like that once more and him shoving my baby sister, I had taken enough. I was taking Rainy and leaving. It was either that or me trying to hurt him and nothing good coming from it." She sucked in a deep breath then moved out of his arms and strode to the fence.

"What happened?" he couldn't help but ask as he followed her.

She stared across the pasture at the open ground and the trees beyond. "I told Rainy to go inside. She knew those words meant hide, and she did as I asked. He was so angry when I told him we were leaving that he swung at me but I moved out of the way. His fury then was clear in his expression but he startled me by turning away and heading to the truck, my so-called mother followed him. He shoved her to the ground when she stumbled into him and then he climbed inside. I was stunned that he was leaving—but I was so wrong.

His old truck was facing me on the rutted driveway and between him and me there was a large oak tree on the side of the drive and unknown to me, Rainy had come out the back door and was now hiding behind it. As he gassed his truck, instead of putting it in reverse and leaving, he blasted toward me—" her eyes filled with tears "—and my bold sister raced from behind that tree screaming and waving her arms as she ran in front of the truck, yelling for him to stop," her voice trembled but she kept talking. "She would have taken the full hit and been dead, but the truck's tires hit a deep rut made from heavy rains and tire tracks and thank God, the front wheel hit it right before the truck reached her, throwing it sideways so it grazed Rainy. *Hard*, but it knocked her—*threw* her to the side instead of running straight over her. She landed on a pile of broken logs, crumbled and silent."

*Rage* whipped through Nicholas, he yanked his hat from his head and slapped it to his thigh—wishing he had this piece of trash man in the grip of his hands.

He had never in his life felt fury like he did right now listening to this caring, beautiful, *hurting* woman.

# CHAPTER TWELVE

Eyes deep behind tears, Emmy's words trembled, her heart clenched and though she didn't look at Nick the whole time she was speaking, she did lift her eyes to him a few times. He had listened intently and his eyes glowed with what she could see was anger and sympathy at the same time. She tried not to let the feel of being in his arms affect her but there was no denying the simple fact that he had come to her, put his arms around her buried his handsome face in her hair.

It had been a moment she had never dreamed about.

She trusted him…and so she'd let it all out.

She had never let herself think that there could be a man out there who could affect her the way Nick affected her. Not just the comfort of being in his arms had sent through her, but knowing he had gone through something similar and understood.

She took a deep, calming breath—she'd needed to get this out in the open. It was good therapy and she could trust him. And so, in the next few moments she continued with a steadier voice telling him everything about how she'd shot and killed her father. And that thankfully, *miraculously*, her sister was still alive.

"I often think how I could be serving time in prison for what I did, yes there had been anger, but also it had been true self-defense. If he'd gotten up, there was no telling who would be dead." As she spoke those words, Nick grimaced and his eyes hardened as did the line of lips. She'd felt it all on that day.

"You both could have been dead," he said, his voice low and gritty.

So true. "I know I should feel guilt. And there's sometimes deep inside that I do, that I wonder if I could have stopped it long before it got to that day, that moment. But I didn't and he tried to kill my sister. Yes, he tried to kill me, but it was my innocent sister who had, for the first time, acted on the anger built inside of her and it had nearly gotten her killed.

"What she had to endure knowing I was taking beatings and trying to protect her filled *her* with anger. I had ignored that until that day and it almost cost me losing her. Now, my anger, my fury, and on that day seeing her limp, twisted body lying there had driven me to react with so much anger that I risked losing her by going to prison for something I might have been able to avoid if I had gotten her out earlier or just told my teacher at school. But I hadn't done that. Thank goodness it was looked at as self-defense. If I had been put in jail she would have lived with guilt, she does now some anyway. She doesn't talk about it but I know it's there, but also, there's determination. It showed that day in the diner when she told me she wanted to ride the horses." Oh, what a moment that had been. "I owe you for giving her that."

"You don't owe me anything. Thank you for trusting me. And I can tell you that *I* feel the anger inside of me at what happened to you and Rainy so I can't even imagine what you felt inside. Yes, all of us abused boys, neglected or forgotten boys have been through rough times. We all deal with it in different ways. You, Emmy Swanson, dealt with it in a sacrificial way. You gave yourself to save your sister in so many ways there's nothing for you to regret. At least that's the way I look at it."

She let the words of this man who she'd begun to admire deeply that first day, drift through her like a gentle caress and as the look in his eyes dove deep into her heart—*no*…

She could *not* let her heart go there.

She couldn't let this emotion she was feeling turn the doorknob of the door to her heart that she had slammed closed years ago. Her heart belonged to making the life of her sister beautiful from now on. She wanted to see Rainy have a life full of joy and happiness. That was *all* she needed to give herself the sunshine she wanted for her own life. Emmy let the determined thought fill her.

She *needed nothing more*, not even this amazing man interrupting her mission ever since her sister crumbled on the ground on that dark day.

*You need nothing more.*

The words echoed through her head again, she'd *lived* for this time ever since that horrible day. Her words were going to be firmer this time, her whole insides had strengthened in those moments with the reminder of what she was here for: To make sure her sister lived the life meant for her.

"Nick,"—*incredible Nick*—"I can't deny your kindness. And that your heart to come back here to your hometown, to give back blessings that you were blessed with is so heart-warming. You are amazing to me and I can't deny telling you how much I admire you. And the fact that you're going to do that for me and my sister, well it's just… you are just a miracle standing here in front of me." She took a breath. "But, I have to say this. And I mean it."

"What?" he asked, stepping toward her.

"I, I felt emotions there in your arms that I've never felt before," she said the words but she did not let her voice tremble as she saw the light jump brighter in his amazing eyes—there was no denying that he felt what she'd felt.

*She had to stop it.* "But Nick, I have to tell you no more. Thank you for letting me get my pain, and my anger, and my love for my sister out in the open. I've never, ever had someone to voice that to and for that I'll always be indebted to you. It's clear and obvious that God has put you in the right spots at the right moment and that Nana knows when it's time to send her men of heart in to help. She knew you were who I needed to talk to and for that I'll always be thankful… but no more. I have to level with you. I know that we shared something, something undeniable, but I *am* denying it. I don't want my heart anywhere other than focused on what I can give my sister. And I don't want to lead you on." There the words were out.

His expression had changed to serious thoughts. It was so evident those amazing eyes of his had darkened. His smile had not turned into a frown but a straight line of deep thought. She just waited. Waited and prayed he didn't say anything that could shake up her determination.

"I get it. Emmy, I do get it.," he said at last. "Your heart is where you want it to be and where you need it to be. I've been there, done that. And though I'll just have to be honest with you, *you* saw through me. You saw something that I was unable to deny and that's that, yes, there's definitely something between us. Something I would like to see grow to fulfillment. I mean, I've never experienced feelings as deep as I'm feeling standing here now talking to you. Wanting to take you in my arms and protect you—and your sister. I want to be that person who shows you that not all men are idiots and beasts. Sweet Nana was the woman in my life who showed me how truly wonderful a woman could be. And Randolph—my true dad of my heart showed me what I needed from a dad who loved me. As he also shows all of his sons, old and younger. These younger boys that are out there walking the streets with Rainy. What I've learned in my life is that what you're given you can pass on and that's what I'm fixin' to do. I'm telling you, I'll never do anything you don't want me to do—but I will help your sister. Me and all of these boys that are excited to take what they've been helped with and move it forward. I won't let the feelings you stir inside of me get in the way of that. Does that sound good to you?"

This man was amazing. She… *admired* him. She *lov*—she cut the word off that had come instantly to her thoughts. She would never allow it to come to her when it came to a man. She loved her sister, loved her dearly and until the day Rainy gave her nieces and nephews to love too, that was it—her heart and life were now lived for Rainy to make up for all the years her being silent had cost them both in that house they should have left earlier.

"Thank you. You're amazing, so you helped me get through that moment and I am so appreciative now I have to walk back up that alley and enjoy watching my sister have a great day."

To her amazement, this fabulous man grinned tipped his hat and cocked his arm. "Sounds like the thing to do. May I escort you down this alley to the sunshine that waits for you when you see your sister smiling?"

She smiled at him. "Yes. To the end of the alley we go."

And at the end of the alley she would let him go— at least this part of him but as they walked slowly down the alley for just that moment she let her heart feel and enjoy the feel of their arms and hearts locked together— something she was never going to let herself feel again.

# CHAPTER THIRTEEN

Sunday morning Nick sat on his back-porch steps watching the soft pink sunrise lifting in the sky, the peaceful sky, far from what he was feeling. He wanted to stay home. It was ridiculous. He had to go to the event at the Sunrise Ranch, the fishing tournament. A great day of reunion with all the fellas he'd hung out with yesterday. But his mind had locked onto his time with Emmy and that's where it stayed. He'd hated leaving her yesterday, but she'd been in control and after he'd held her hand and they'd walked down the alley he'd released it—released her just as she'd wanted. She stepped forward and spotted her sister down the street and without hesitating she'd left him standing there, and went where her heart was…with her sister. Rainy was sitting in the fold-up chair Tony had carried on his back and now the guys all surrounded her talking and laughing, making sure she was having fun.

His brothers who he loved, and was so proud of at that moment. They were giving what they'd learned from the beloved ranch and one woman's dream for them. Lydia's dream had come true. They were passing her dream of love on and he didn't even have to look at Emmy's face to know she saw it too. He knew she'd felt in her heart that her sister would get the care and support she needed here and Rainy was getting exactly what Emmy had hoped for.

Now, he pushed a rock with the toe of his boot and looked across the pastures with the sun rising in front of him but not inside. He'd wanted to take Emmy back into his arms, to tell her that life was going to be good from now on.

That she could open her heart up—instead he'd said her name and when she had looked at him with those eyes shining, he tipped his hat and said he would be around if she needed him.

And so be it. Today, he was going to go be with his

brothers who'd come home for the weekend and then he'd get back to business. He was going to help her sister walk again. What he saw in Rainy's eyes was not defeat but the shine of a new day. She was determined to walk or become the best possible, with his and Wes's help—so, what in the heck was he doing sitting here on his porch?

He stood up, straightened the Stetson he had had for years, a gift from his father, Randolph McDermott. His words when he had given Nicholas this hat had been, "Be the man you are meant to be, lead the way."

So be it. No more sidetracking, he would get this done.

He had been sidetracked to get back at those who had left him behind, but now he was on the right track, this was where he was going to make a difference and it started with Rainy—not Emmy.

Today they were fishing at the enormous lake down the hill, he smiled thinking about Chili and Drewbaker. The barrel was coming out today. A grinning Wes had said he was heading out early this morning to help load the eight-foot, round cattle trough onto the trailer. Then he was going to unload it at the lake this morning, for whenthe fishing began.

And that was where Nicholas needed to be, there in time to help roll that round metal water trough down that hill if they needed him. It would be fun, he had to remind himself that was the way life was supposed to be, yeah serious moments, but also enjoyable moments, and he was going to enjoy watching what went on today.

A few minutes later Nicholas drove to the spot on the ranch where everything was already set up and people were gathering. His brothers Morgan, Tucker, and Rowdy stood on the side of the hill watching all their other brothers launching their boats into the lake.

As he walked to stand beside them on the hill, they grinned at him and then looked back down as Wes pulled his truck to a halt beside the lake. On the trailer he was pulling sat the big round water trough.

"Those two are going to have a good time today and we're going to enjoy watching them," he said, knowing it was true.

"Yes, we are," Morgan agreed. "I always remember that first time they did this. Wes was with them so I'm glad he's helping once again."

Tucker frowned. "Those two did really well last time in that tub but they're getting older and might have trouble maneuvering that massive tub around. We're going to have to really watch them."

Rowdy punched his sheriff brother. "Whoa, Tucker, you know that thing won't sink. But if it makes you feel better, I went yesterday afternoon and made sure there were no leaks, so relax it's going to be a good day."

In that moment Nicholas saw Rainy walk slowly from behind the truck, pushing her walker in front of her. "What's Rainy doing down there?" He took a step forward.

"Hold on, dude," Rowdy said. "Wes and Tony will take good care of her. She rode with them in the truck pulling the trailer, and Drewbaker and Chili were right behind them. They're all going to make sure she's okay."

His brothers were looking at him, and he knew what they were seeing. They were seeing a guy who was showing maybe a little too much emotion. "I'm going to help her with riding the horses, but the last thing I want is to see her get hurt today."

Morgan stared hard at him. "Don't you think she needs to feel like she can do what she wants to do? Just because she's on that walker doesn't mean she can't do anything."

"You're right," he said, knowing it was true.

"After all, her sister let her ride with them," Rowdy pointed out.

Morgan nodded. "Yeah, she did. Emmy called Jolie last night and asked her if she thought it would be okay for Rainy to do this. Jolie told her that Wes and Tony would take care of her and Drewbaker and Chili would too. Obviously, Emmy didn't tell her not to ride with him. So, she's down there right now earning the satisfaction that she's in control and can do something."

"Right," Nicholas agreed. He knew she had to get self-confidence in herself. And he knew that those three fellas down there, young and old, would be on watch for her.

What got him the most was that Emmy hadn't called and asked his advice. Instead, she'd called Jolie and everyone had known Rainy was going to help with the boat but him. He'd been left on the sidelines. Emmy was telling him in this way that they weren't connected. And that slammed him in the gut like a punch by Tucker, one of the strongest, muscled Marines there had ever been.

"You okay?" Rowdy asked, his adventurous brother was studying him hard.

"Yeah, I am. I'm just here to help her learn to walk and Emmy is—" he looked at his brothers and their knowing gazes. They knew what they were seeing. "Hold on, guys, no romance is happening there. And I can't say anything other than Emmy has her priorities and it all has to do with her little sister. I'm going to help her ride and hopefully build strength so that Emmy can watch her walk without that walker one day."

Tucker slapped a wide hand on his shoulder and gave him a grip of encouragement. "Hang in there, brother. They always have to get their mind set, build their strength, and you have to let them. Believe me, I know. But, like me, there was never anything better feeling than when I watched my comrades succeed in the battle they were fighting. You are going to help that girl succeed in the battle she's fighting. And you're also going to help Emmy too. We don't know everything, but we know she's fighting too."

He nodded, because it was true. Emmy was fighting her own fight.

The silver round tank, standing on its side, rolled off the trailer and everyone rolled it into the water. There, they let it fall flat in the water which instantly sent a huge splash over those standing close. Everyone, including Rainy, laughed and clapped their hands. At that moment Rainy let go of her walker as she clapped, holding her balance for an instant before she clasped the handles once again.

Rainy knew her limits and pushed them in excitement and that was a great sign. She would have to push her limits in order to achieve more improvements. *He* was going to have to push her but pushing herself was most important and watching her now gave him assurance that she was here to achieve her goal.

But what about Emmy? He glanced around, she wasn't with them but he knew she was there somewhere, watching. He spotted her on the far side of the group of ladies who were loading the tables with refreshments. She stood at the far end, her arms locked tightly against her ribs, her hands gripping her elbows. Tension radiated from her, she wasn't moving; she wasn't talking…just watching.

And he had a feeling she was praying—or *worrying*.

# CHAPTER FOURTEEN

Emmy stood frozen, watching down the hill to the large lakeside and her sister walking on her walker with Wes, Tony, and the fishermen Chili and Drewbaker. Wes and Tony had both promised her they'd take care of Rainy.

Rainy had nicely but firmly told her she was going.

In that instant Emmy had realized things were not in her control. Her sister was seventeen years old. She was in control of her life now, which she had a right to do—after all, Emmy hadn't been in her life that much. Not really, yes, she had gone and visited as much as she could, but her sister had been under the supervision of someone else. She'd had no say in her sister's life after they had put her in the foster home. And in the moment, she'd told Emmy she was going to watch them put the tin water trough in the water, told her in her nice way, it had been her letting Emmy know she was now her own boss.

Emmy had to be glad about that—she rubbed her forehead—she was glad. Happy they were together, thrilled that her little sister was determined to make her own way, and that *included* calling the shots on what she did and didn't do.

Now, here Emmy stood on the hillside helping set up the tables—she was supposed to be helping when in fact, she was standing here watching Rainy watch the guys get Chili and Drewbaker's odd fish tub into the lake. Emmy had to admit she wanted to see it too, she just hadn't known she would have to watch her sister pushing her walker around on its wheels beside the tub.

"She's doing good down there," Miss Jo said as she stepped up beside her. "One thing about that little gal, she's got control of that walker, but I know it's got to be hard on you. Worry is written all over your face."

She knew it was true. "I'm torn up inside. It's taken me all these years to get us back together like a family should be. However, I'm having to let her go at the same time. So, it's rough. But I'm going to do it, she has a right to call the shots in her own life now."

Miss Jo gave her a squeeze around the waist, the short little lady's head came to about Emmy's shoulder, but she was strong in her hug. "You're going to do it, girlfriend. And have confidence, because those boys are intent on helping her. Especially those two, Wes and Tony. They've got hearts of gold and they've both been through a lot, but they're give-back fellas. They want to give back just like that wonderful Nicholas and the other men have done for them."

"They both seem wonderful and so caring."

"I knew when I first got to know Nicholas that he would be wonderful. He came early and like Wes and Tony, he pushed things back behind closed doors. He hid it all and yet he stepped out and tried to help every boy who came to the ranch and I knew one day his calling would be exactly that in some form. I knew Wes was going to come back to town eventually too. That boy helped so many in his life here but he thought being a champion bull rider was going to make everything good. Just like Nicholas thought working hard and using that big wise brain of his was going to make things right when he made all those millions. Which he did, yet here he is just like I thought he would be. And then there's Tony. Special Tony, one of those who has been through the worst of the worst, and yet he's never hesitated. He knew his life was here on Sunrise Ranch, giving hope and love to all the boys who came here over the years and those yet to come. They're all special."

"Yes, they are," she said, almost whispered. They truly were special, including Nick.

"Now you can talk to Nana about this but they all didn't give in to Tony wanting to live here forever. Because they care about him, they were trying to push him to go on out into the world when the time comes and not hide because of his outward scars. They thought if he didn't go out and start a new life but stayed at the ranch it would be like a shelter for him. They didn't want him using the shelter as a hiding place."

Emmy's heart tugged tight.

"They wanted him to go out in the world and test it out. But, for all I know, that boy told them in his own gentle, but firm way that he was going to be like Chet and stay here on the ranch. Chet wasn't okay with that at first but now he is, he recognizes that like him, staying here and helping others is his calling and makes him happy. Joining his older adoptive brothers' team will be a great addition. I'm telling you this because it's about the drive inside of a person. The drive that sets them apart. Your sister has it too, just like Wes and Tony. And just like you do."

Heart thundering Emmy looked at Miss Jo. "If I only had that drive early on I could have saved her from all she's going through now."

Miss Jo reached her hand out again and grabbed her forearm. She squeezed hard—that tiny hand could make the greatest pies in the world and it had a hard grip on her now, drilling into her as her gentle eyes touched her with a firm look. "Your life has a plan, Emmy. No matter what you went through or got through, there's a plan. Sadly, some people's lives are harder than others but it all comes down to who you've got inside of you. And how *you* want or choose to use what you've been through to help others. Those fellas there want to help others. Your sister included."

She stared at the little lady, took a deep breath, letting Miss Jo's words sink in. Her gaze went back to Wes and Tony, then to Drewbaker and Chili. They were all smiling as the silver barrel reached the water. Wes tipped it into the water and there it floated. And her happy sister took her hands off the walker, lifted them into the air and shook them as she squealed.

It was an awesome sight seeing the momentary freedom Rainy had standing on her own. Emmy's heart squeezed tight with joy watching her excitement. Then, her frail body grew unstable, and she started toppling toward the ground. Like a lightning bolt Tony—though further away from her than Wes—dove across the grass, skidded on his knees to her side and gently helped her as she struggled to get up. He lifted her to a sitting position then gently pushed her hair from her face.

Emmy's heart roared, and she made the move to go to Emmy's side but tiny Miss Jo tightened her grip on her arm.

"Let Tony help her. She doesn't need her sister racing to her side. She'll get this and look at Tony.

That's what he knows his life is for, helping and look at Wes, he's on standby but knows when to stand back. If there are two people who can help her get stronger, it's those two. Those two old fellas know what they're doing too, they knew she would be safe if not with them, then with Wes and Tony. So big sister, just relax and watch as caring, strong Tony helps her up. I have to say they look like Elvis Presley and Cinderella."

Tears sprang to Emmy's eyes—*Cinderella*. Tears and a chuckle too as she watched the handsome Elvis Presley look-a-like and her beautiful Cinderella sister smile.

Oh, what a combination.

And then Rainy took hold of the walker set in front of her and that smart Wes knew Tony needed to help her. Tony, the boy who was a walking miracle from all that he'd gone through. And her sweet sister—delete, delete her brain yelled, backspacing so she could replace sweet with strong. Her *strong* sister could and would do the same as Tony.

All three of them, Tony and Wes, each on Rainy's side, were now headed toward the edge of the water. Her eyes took in what they had unloaded from the truck earlier, five lawn chairs, five fishing rods, and five life vests.

Her brain faltered suddenly seeing what she'd not observed earlier, five of everything, including five life vests—*why?*

* * *

Nicholas had watched what was going on at the lake while glancing to see the troubled expressions on Emmy's face. When Rainy fell, Miss Jo had held Emmy back. Knowing Miss Jo was helping Emmy, his gaze had gone back to the scene by the water's edge and he'd stepped forward to go help, but in a flash there was Tony racing to the rescue. The cowboy slid on his knees to reach her. Now, Nicholas watched him help Rainy sit up and then, the two worked together, no tears, no frowns, just smiles and determination getting her to a standing position.

On her feet, Rainy held tight to Tony's arms getting steady then, boom, she let go, he went to help Wes and as if nothing had happened she went back to rooting the guys on as they loaded the silver, tin cup with fishing gear…lawn chairs with the rubber grips on the bottom for no slipping, rods, life vests—his gaze went back to the chairs and the vest. Five chairs and five life vests— five each. Instantly he headed down the hill. What were they thinking?

In that same moment he glimpsed someone else hurrying down the hill and knew instantly who it was, so he picked up his pace to intercept Emmy. "Slow down. Yeah I know you want to get down there and me too. But, the last thing you need to do is roll down this steep hill, it's a lot steeper than it looks."

She didn't slow down just gave him a glare then focused on her target at the base of the hill.

He was glad he'd gotten to her because it was a steep hill, she just didn't realize it and if she fell at least he would be here to help her not roll the rest of the way down.

"This makes me angry," she growled, breathless. "I was trying to cope with letting her do her thing, and I know I have to, but she has no business being out there in that water."

They reached solid ground near the trough that was now half on ground and half in the water, with Tony standing inside. Wes had just picked Rainy up and was handing her to Tony who took her gently in his arms then placed her in a chair that was waiting for her. Thankfully, she already had her life vest on.

"What are y'all doing?" he asked, his voice firmer than he wanted it to be but that's how he felt inside. What *were* they doing? Thinking?

All eyes came to him and Emmy, who was silent—probably fighting back tears.

Chili stepped forward. "We're goin' on a fishin' trip. We'll be just off the bank here, and this big ole bucket of confidence won't sink. I promise you," he said, looking at Emmy. "She wanted to go and the boys wanted to go with her, so here we are."

"But—" Emmy started but Rainy broke in.

"I'm glad I'm in here, Emmy, don't get so upset. I already told you I'm going to be stepping forward. I will not be afraid. I love you dearly, sis, and I thank you for worrying about me. However, that will not stop me from experiencing life. I've been holed up all these years and I consider myself a free woman now. So, whether or not you like it I'm going in this little silver boat."

"I promise we'll take care of her," Wes said.

Tony had his hand on Rainy's shoulder. "We won't let anything happen to her. I swim like a fish, Wes does too. She's got a life vest on and this solid metal fish tank won't even break so we're going to be fine. And then there's Chili and Drewbaker, they might be old but they're not stupid and won't let anything happen to us. From what I've heard, they've swam in many a lakes and ponds growing up themselves."

"Yes, we have," Drewbaker drawled.

Chili grinned. "You bet we have, and one of them rivers down there is pretty rough and yet we were able to do it back in the day. When you're living life, you've got to experiment some." His gaze locked with Emmy's, and Nicholas' gaze went to her.

Emmy's expression was one of realization. He wanted to reach out and pat her shoulder like Tony was patting Rainy's, but he held back. She didn't want that from him.

"I have no say in it, obviously," she said, her words stiff and resigned. "Just be careful. Rainy, I want you to live your life like you want to, sometimes it's just going to be hard for me. So, don't be mad."

Rainy gave a gentle smile. "You're doing great. You always were the strong one, I'm just following in your footsteps."

Emmy nodded, locking her arms together across her ribs—probably to keep from reaching for her sister.

Nicholas wasn't taking it too well. He was going to have a talk with Wes and Tony when this was over, but right now it wasn't for him to say. He'd been shut out. "Y'all be careful," was all he said, then because he wanted to reach out and take Emmy's hand in his, he turned and headed back up the hill.

If he hadn't done that, he would have taken her hand and walked her back and she didn't want that from him. It was obvious. Even if she might need it—what was he thinking? She didn't need him and she'd made that very clear.

\* \* \*

Emmy made it back up to the table where she could be with the ladies. They greeted her with hugs as she fought back tears and was glad she didn't cry.

Mabel tightened her hug. "You hang in there, my dear. You're going to get as strong as that determined little sister of yours. You're already strong because you turned and walked back up that hill. Y'all, just keep going, it's going to be alright and I have to tell you I'm proud of Tony and Wes. They see her determination and those are two strong boys who are going to make sure she stays safe." She smiled. "Tony and Wes are strong, she's safe. Now, turn around and look, they're pushing off. Look at the smile on your sister's face."

Emmy turned and saw Wes sitting in his chair on one side of Rainy as he pushed off with his oar. Drewbaker and Chili, who were sitting on the far side of the tub, paddled with their long paddles. Tony sat on the other side of her sister and pushed also, but even though all that was going on, Emmy's eyes were on her sister. Her brilliantly smiling, happy, *thrilled* sister. Tears welled in Emmy's eyes and her heart—"Look at her, I think she feels free." She gasped the last words out and her cheeks were wet with tears.

"That's an interesting word you're using," Edwina said, coming up carrying a stack of pie boxes. She set them on the table and looked at Emmy. "That little sister of yours is going to push her limits. She's going to touch the moon one day and so are you. To be honest, I'm kind of learning from watching her."

"What are you learning, Edwina?" Miss Jo asked.

Edwina put her hands on her thin hips and that stern face of hers lightened up. "I'm learning that no matter what crud life has dealt me, or any of us, we get back up and push hard. I mean, look at her." She nodded to Rainy on the silver tub surrounded by her friends.

"What are you afraid of?" Emma asked, baffled. "You're one strong lady. You do what you need to do, what you want to do and nobody takes anything off of you. You don't let anybody get away with anything, so what in your life are you learning from my little sister?" Emmy was learning from Edwina because Edwina was so strong. She wanted Rainy to learn from Edwina. She was—or at least had thought about it because from what she learned, Edwina had been through a lot and this woman took nothing from anyone.

Edwina looked at her, that smile was still on her face. "I'm learning that sometimes you don't need to be afraid of what you are afraid of. You need to learn from your mistakes and take a step out. Right now, she's taking a big step out just floating on that water."

Her words stunned Emmy. "But you are one of the strongest people I know. I've heard stories of how you yanked somebody up and forced them out the door when you had to."

Edwina grinned bigger than Emmy had ever seen her grin. "Yup, I've done that and that man I did it to was sitting in the diner with you the day you came in to tell the ladies about your sister. Nicholas came in and was sitting at the table near his while all that conversation was going on."

Emmy's eyebrows met, then looked around to see if any of the ladies knew who she was talking about. To her surprise all the ladies had curious looks in their eyes as they stared at Edwina.

"He still comes in?"

"Yes, he does. The diner has the best food in the twenty counties surrounding it, so yes, it gives me the power to get what I want."

"It was that Larson, yes, that was his name. That

big, tall cowboy who sat down there and asked Nick a couple of questions?"

Edwina frowned. "Yep, and when I got ready to go, he stuck his big booted foot out in front of me."

Emmy remembered it distinctly. Though she had her mind on Nick at that time and his questions about Rainy, she remembered the way the big cowboy had watched Edwina walk away.

Interesting. *Very interesting.*

That tough looking cowboy. "So you like physically threw that big guy out of the diner?" Edwina chuckled, as did everybody. "Well yeah, but I have to admit part of it was that he wasn't fighting back because he was so stunned I was attempting to do what I did. And since he started coming back, he don't do that kind of stuff anymore except every once in awhile, like that day he tried to halt me by sticking his boot out."

She just stared at Edwina thinking back on that moment she had been distracted by everything else that was going on. "So what are we talking about now? I'm confused."

Edwina laughed. "We're talking about sometimes

you do things in response and that's how I react. I had to toughen up through my bad marriages and my bad dudes I've made mistakes with. I toughen up by finally putting up steel walls around my heart and attitude and knuckles on my fist. I've lived like that all these years but I help whoever I can with my attitude; however the truth is, I'm not real sure after watching all this falling in love that's been happening around me and seeing these young boys and your sister overcoming far worse than I experienced…well it has me thinking. Maybe I need to let some of my fists come down and let all I've learned from my mistakes help me find the right guy. You know, maybe time to dip my toes back in the water. I never dreamed I would even think about it after Lester, Darwin, and then Marv. Nope not happenin' but then, I started watch'n and learnin—"

Gasps erupted around her at those words.

"You want to find a *man*?" Mabel was the first to ask.

"Really, that's what you want?" Miss Jo asked, her expression one of shock.

"I think this is great." Nana walked over and put her

hand on Edwina's arm, patting it in her gentle way. "I'm going to start praying for the right man to come into your life. I think that would be awesome. Me, after I lost my wonderful hubby that I loved so very much and was so blessed with, can't take that step forward. Even though we all know there is one man in this town who is wonderful and sends me flowers a lot."

Emmy was lost. Obviously, it read on her face because Miss Jo leaned over and whispered, "It's Chili. He's been sending her flowers ever since Suzie moved to town and opened her flower shop. Sending her flowers and letting her know that he has feelings for her, but she doesn't acknowledge it."

Shockwaves riveted through Emmy. All this was going on around her and she didn't even know it. She looked down on the lake and spotted Rainy laughing— her little sister had a fish on the end of her fishing pole and was excited.

Emmy's heart did a triple leap at the excitement and she stood there with all that going on around her and watched her little sister reeling in the fish as Tony and Wes stood beside her in the silver tub and Drewbaker and Chili grinned.

"Well, Edwina," she said, tearing her gaze off her little sister and looking at the tough woman. "I guess sometimes when we've made bad mistakes, we put our shields up and we don't want to let it down." She sighed. "But sometimes it's time."

Edwina smiled. "Yup that's the lesson I'm learning and I hope you are too. I'm not saying I'm going to, but well, I have had a few notes delivered to me at times asking if I'd like to go out—"

More gasps erupted around them.

"You *have*?" Miss Jo asked. "At the diner and you didn't even tell me? Edwina, that's wonderful."

"Miss Jo, I'm the waitress at the diner and I keep everybody in line, and yes, as weird as it sounds, with my temperament, I do get notes sometimes. Most I chuck in the garbage after I give the dudes a glare."

"You mean it's been more than *one*?" Nana asked, grinning widely.

"Oh my word, this is so exciting," Mabel said. "Now you've got to tell us if you've been throwing most of them in the trash, then *whose* notes have you kept?"

"Well, little ladies," she drawled. "I ain't lettin' that out just yet, but I'm going to be thinking about it. I ain't saying I'm going to, so don't take me up on that— Well crud now that I've told y'all I'd be a big chicken if I don't go out with this cowboy whose note I've kept." Her expression was tight.

Emmy's heart raced, *goodness gracious*. "Are you going to tell us who the lucky man's going to be?"

Edwina grinned. "Nope, y'all think I'm a big chicken if I don't. But if that little gal down there amongst all those fellas sitting in that rinky-dink tin watering trough out there on the water can smile like that when she caught that tiny fish, then I've got to do what I've got to do." And with that Edwina turned and walked away.

Emmy's gaze went around as Nana, Miss Jo, and Mabel were all grinning as they watched her leave.

And the question was: *Wow*, who was Edwina going to go out with?

# CHAPTER FIFTEEN

It had been a great weekend for the town, for his brothers, their families and their kids. Nicholas concentrated on that as he stood beside Rainy's horse to help her get in the saddle. He didn't focus on how Emmy didn't want him in her life.

Today was about helping Rainy. Wes had already settled Rainy into her saddle and she was actually very excited to get out of the arena today. He and Wes had talked about the route they would take and had agreed on the same route, it was smooth and beautiful. Today it was about safety and fun. Rainy needed to see that being handicapped by her accident didn't mean she had to sit on the sidelines. She was going to love getting out in the open fields. Like she'd enjoyed catching the fish from inside of the tub.

Now, he had to help Emmy get into the saddle for the first time. This was going to be an uncomfortable moment. He and Wes would both be looking out for her since she'd never ridden, but he had entrusted Wes with Rainy. It was clear that Wes felt protective of her and would be beside her all the way. And as much as Nicholas wanted to put distance between him and Emmy, he needed to be beside her on this ride.

Needed to make sure she was safe and comfortable since she would be on the horse for the first time. That, and also worrying about her sister as they traveled across the pasture for the first time. He reminded himself that this new endeavor of his wasn't just for disabled kids and young adults; it was also for the ones who were trying to adapt to their situations. The ones who were by their side as they adapted too.

So he reminded himself that his new job required him to be near Emmy. He tried to push the other things that bothered him to the back rack. He also tried to push aside that fact as he told her to put her boot in the stirrup, he placed his hand on her lower back—for support, to give her assurance that he was there by her side. But the sensation that raced up his arm just from that small touch sent his world galloping.

The glance she gave him the moment his fingertips touched her back told him that as much as she wanted to deny it, she felt it too.

*Get it together.* He had to be in control here.

He had to show her he wasn't in this to get in her way.

So, he gave her a light smile of assurance. "I'm just here to make sure you can get in the saddle without problems. Then we ride and enjoy watching your sister put a bigger smile on her face than she has right now."

Emmy's gaze went from him to where her sister sat in her saddle, grinning at Wes, who sat straight and controlled in his saddle. She looked at him then. "I feel assured that she will be safe, so thank you."

"You're welcome, it's going to be a great day and we're going to make sure you enjoy it too." He tried to keep any type of feelings of attraction out of his voice and his eyes. However, he couldn't control his blasted eyes—and he saw her falter as their gazes locked—no telling what she saw in them before she ripped hers away. She focused on the saddle horn as she hoisted herself to a standing position, one foot in the stirrup and the other needing to be shot over the back of the horse and into the stirrup on the other side. She'd done good so far, doing as he'd instructed her, and without any problem the next instant her other leg was over the saddle, her boot in the stirrup and she settled into the seat.

"How was that?" she asked.

"It was perfect. You are going to be a natural horse rider." She was, it was easy to see.

"I'm not so sure about that, but after watching you with my sister and Wes too, y'all have made good examples showing me how to get in this saddle. How to hold the reins and hopefully I can do your instructions justice."

A small grin came in reaction to her words and he held back the big one he wanted to give her. Not thinking, he patted her knee. "So, settle in while I saddle up and then we'll get this show on the road."

And that's just what they did. He mounted his

horse, showed her how to move her horse with just a little nudge of her knees or heels against its sides. She did exactly as instructed. He smiled at Wes and Rainy, who were smiling too, also happy Emmy connected so well with her horse.

"Alright, you two, let's head out. It's going to be a great day. Either of you feel worried or like you're needing help in the saddle, that's what Wes and I are here for, just let us know."

"I feel steady in this saddle and ready to head out." Rainy grinned at them and she looked steady, her posture good in the saddle. She was able to almost actually sit up straight because her hip wasn't yanking her to the side, it was settled securely beneath her in the saddle. It was when she was trying to walk that her hip was trouble. He liked the fact that she sat there and smiled and looked absolutely normal and strong.

His gaze went from her back to Emmy who, to his surprise, was looking at him with tears glistening in her eyes.

"Thank you," she said as they started riding. "She

looks so full of life right now."

He said nothing, instead he glanced at her hands and the reins, making sure she was doing it right. It gave him a moment to push the emotion that her eyes shot to his heart under control.

"She's going to be great. And Wes and I are really glad that we're able to help her. You did right, letting her be involved in this."

She focused on Wes and her sister riding ahead of them, keeping her eyes off of him. Helpful, since when her eyes were on him, his insides twisted.

She glanced at him then looked away. "This is wonderful. I've never ridden a horse and I'm actually very proud I'm being able to ride like this. It's partly because you chose the right horse for me, or let the guys choose the right horse for me. You've prepared me and I feel happy."

His heart was raging. "Good, like I said, that's what I want." He didn't let his mind go to what would really make him happy with this woman. This beautiful woman who was driving his heart and dreams to the edge of wanting, needing something he feared he would never get…Emmy's love.

She reserved that for her sister and no one else.

* * *

Rainy knew her sister was riding behind her watching, worrying. She had no idea that Rainy's heart had never felt so full as it did in this moment, riding on this horse, in a saddle that fit her perfectly. Her weekend fishing had caused friction but she'd loved it. She'd felt free.

Now, here, she was riding her horse across this smooth pasture feeling almost like a normal person—no she *did* feel like a normal person. Her back was straight, she didn't even have to lean into the back of the saddle as she held her spine straight. The ache in her hip wasn't so bad, because the pressure wasn't fully on her foot, knee or hip.

Riding in this saddle was steady feeling rather than unsteady like she had worried it would be. She knew if they kept this up that riding in a regular saddle was a possibility, not needing her legs strapped or needing the back support behind her. But, if she was wrong it didn't matter—she was riding a *horse* across a pasture with a beautiful countryside in front of her, ready to be explored.

She glanced at Wes, the strong cowboy riding beside her, and he was grinning. "Why are you smiling like that?"

"I know how you're feeling. Freedom."

Her heart yanked. "Exactly. I haven't felt freedom since the day I saw my…the man who was supposed to be my father slammed his fist into my sister's shoulder blade. I was five when I first saw it, or remember seeing it happen. Emmy had taught me to get in the hiding place she had shown me when my—that man—started yelling. And I always did what she told me. But on that day I snuck out to see what she always wanted to hide from me. I cried when she flew to the floor and her eyes locked with mine and I saw worry in them—not pain. *Worry* for *me* rose over her pain, so I spun and ran to hide like she'd taught me.

"I was young but knew how much I meant to her and from that day forward I always did what she told me. She was trying to protect me with everything she had and even at five years old, I knew the love she had for me. Trying to protect me from what she endured…" Her voice wavered, but she fought back the tears. "Love, *true* love shined in her gaze."

"I'm so sorry you went through that," Wes growled.

"Me too. She sent me where I belonged for that time, that age of not understanding. She took what I might not have been able to endure at that young age. Like Jesus, she sacrificed for me. But, in my mind, I knew I couldn't hide forever. And that day came when I was about to turn eight. I couldn't take it anymore. I was old enough to know a bruise when I saw it. And I knew where it came from. Bruises and cuts she hid with shirts and pants. But that day." She paused.

"It's okay, I understand."

"That day," she continued. "I couldn't take it anymore was the day I saw her telling them she was taking me away. She'd sent me to my hiding place but I came out the back of the house and hid behind a tree. I heard her telling him and my drunk mother her plans. That's when he got in his truck and gassed it—I couldn't take it any longer. I ran out shouting at him and he hit me before he would have hit her." She growled out the last words, her heart still so full of anger at the people who were supposed to love her but instead had other ideas. "Emmy, sweet Emmy was the one who loved me and I loved her too."

Wes stared at her, pain in his eyes. She spoke before he could, "So, here I am today riding this horse because I didn't die. But for the first time in my life I tried to take up for the girl who'd always taken up for me. I had heard her words to him, she was taking me away. We were going to leave and live free—and that piece of trash didn't like it." Her words were harsh so she took a breath, getting a grip. "So, this new journey of ours began. But Wes, it was Emmy's love for me that brought me through everything. I think your bull riding got you through the bad times and horse riding helped you and the others, giving you the peace I see in your eyes right now. And now I feel that peace too. I feel free."

Handsome, muscular, rodeo champion Wes grinned. "I think you, Rainy Swanson, can see everything. But your words, and riding on that horse beside me right now, have shown me where *my* future is. Not riding bulls but helping others find steadiness, happiness…" His gaze dug deep. "And determination to take what you have and make the best of it. To let your strength shine through and to spread that to those you can help."

Rainy's heart throbbed with the beat of the horse's steps and the understanding that she had played a minor role in helping this amazing guy find his meaning. "Well, you are helping me realize we take what we've got and we strive for the best. That's exactly what I'm going to do. You've helped your brothers in many ways. And yes, I know I'm a girl, but like Tony and you did for me, I'm going to help too. Everybody says that no one really knows what you, Wes, went through. I ask and nobody says they know, that all you ever did was hold yours in and help them get through theirs. I can tell Tony admires you."

Wes said nothing for a minute but she saw his hand tighten on his reins as he stared ahead. "What happened to me is what led me to every moment in my life as it is these days. I don't plan on dwelling on it anymore. And the fact that I don't need to get on the back of a raging bull anymore means a lot. That I can find peace in this saddle watching you overcome makes my heart feel happier than it's ever felt before. Rainy, you're going to do great. You have been through a lot, could have been through a lot more if it hadn't been for that amazing sister of yours. You are going to make a difference. Me too. But I can tell you, Tony has been through so much more than I can imagine and he is a walking, talking testament. He's a number one winner with his ability to step out early and start trying to help every foster boy who came into this ranch. He's amazing."

"I knew that from the first moment I heard about him."

"Yeah, everyone sees it. He told our older brothers earlier on that he was going to spend the rest of his life at Sunrise Ranch helping all those who came to live there. He said that was his destiny, not payback to that demon of a man who burned him, scarred him, beat the living daylights out of him. No, his payback was helping others overcome. *Unlike him,* I never knew if I could have figured out my meaning in life quite so certain as he did."

Rainy's heart swelled. "The moment I first heard about Tony, I was drawn to his strength, his heart. And since I've met him, I see it and I'm determined that I'm going to follow in his and your footsteps. I hear that Tony, early on like you said was able to overcome his pain. How did he do it so young?"

Wes looked like his mind went deep and she admired that about the man. He wasn't one to just blurt things out, he really thought it out. Sometimes the thought process went fast, sometimes it went slower.

"He doesn't focus on *his* pain but that of others. Helping makes him stronger."

"Yes, I think you're right." She was going to let things settle inside and make sure she said things right like Wes had just done. She was glad to have this awesome young man to help her see where she was going.

But her mind was on Tony. Tony drew her like no other person ever had. She had just turned seventeen and was her own boss now, and liked it but she knew she wasn't ready for any romance. Still, as much as this handsome, strong Wes meant to her, she knew Tony drew her more. Tony drew her more than anyone she had ever been around.

He made her think about a future that might include him—something she'd never thought about before. Now, sitting here in the saddle, thoughts raced through her causing her heart to waver—she looked at Wes, who was studying her. Suddenly she knew, "Tony helped you, didn't he? His strength in handling everything he's been through is amazing."

"Yes, he did." Wes's expression was serious. "You look at him with his shirt on, the muscles he's built and the stance he takes on holding tight to helping others. It's his way of giving back. It's his calling. That's the only word I can say other than it's his ministry. He quietly reaches out and helps. He even helped Lucy, Rowdy's wife. She was scarred terribly from being in a fire. When she first came to the ranch, I hadn't gone to college yet so was living there full-time. We helped clean her yard when she moved in and she always wore long-sleeved shirts that buttoned at the wrist and to the neck. There was a morning when we helped her and surprised her and she hadn't buttoned her shirt up all the way. We spotted a scar right below where the collar would have covered it up. We didn't say anything because she quickly buttoned it up and we knew she was hiding it."

Rainy's thoughts went to the scars she hadn't seen on Tony but knew were there. Her heart ached for him and for Lucy. "What happened?"

"Tony was quieter than he is now. He didn't talk about what happened to him, he still doesn't talk about it a lot. He rode horses a whole lot, got his peace on the back of a horse. Even then, he helped everyone, even young like that, he knew he could help Lucy. From what we learned later he went and saw her, showed her his scars and told her she would be okay. He still doesn't take his shirt off around everybody, he doesn't mind if you know he's got scars but to show them, he won't do it unless he can help someone by seeing them. He deals with them his own way. But, Rainy, I think he believes he'll never find someone to love him with those scars on him. So, he puts his heart and soul into helping everybody else and is striving to keep his heart locked away."

The words struck her hard. She had just been around for a short time and she already figured out that he put everybody before himself. And that drew her to him, she couldn't deny it.

She saw the concern for him in Wes's expression. "I see that too. I feel like he's going to make a humongous difference in even more lives than he's already made. This is his calling. That sounds kind of strange doesn't it, to be from a life that was bad and then having a calling to help others like Tony has and you too, Wes. But that's what I'm going to do too. So, thank you for helping me know my path. But, there's more, I'm just going to tell you—I kind of feel like I'm here to help Tony."

Wes smiled, his eyes lit up. "That's *exactly* what I've been thinking. I've never seen him look at anyone the way he looks at you. I'm not assuming anything, but, Tony is one of the best people I know and I'd like him to be happier than he thinks he deserves to be. He helps so many, and with what you're telling me, you have quickly jumped to the top of the line too. You're going to be good, you see things and your heart is in the right place. I like that you see Tony as the special guy that he is. But I'm going to warn you, I want you to be careful. I don't want you or Tony getting hurt."

She really loved this guy. "I promise you I'm going to tread lightly and have fun showing Tony that scars inside or outside aren't what keeps us from finding a full life. Look at me, if I never walk completely upright I'm okay with that. Sitting straight on this horse's back makes me happy." Not wanting to mess up she paused. "Wes, I'm not saying that I'm in love with Tony, I'm just saying I have never been drawn to anyone like I am to him. I'd never do anything to mess his life up. Right now, I just know that I want to help here at this ranch. I want to help you and Tony and anyone else who needs help to move forward. And I'm thankful that my sister found this place to start my life over."

Without saying a word, as their horses moved side by side Wes lifted his hand, she lifted hers and they slapped their hands together in a happy high five.

Wes grinned "You, Rainy, are going to be

awesome. And from the sidelines I'll be watching and hoping that if it's meant to be, you can help Tony at least know, that some people, even women, can look past physical scars and see the person inside. That's what Rowdy did with Lucy. And look at them now, they're amazing and happy. They inspire me. Yes, I had my own bad times and now I'm moving forward just like I've been shown." He grinned at her.

She sighed. "All I can tell you, cowboy, is that one day you're going to make some woman's heart happy. In a different way than you're making all these people around you happy. And I can't wait to see who that will be."

He grinned and shook his head. "Whoa, I had no idea that when we got on this horse today you were going to go into all this. I thought this ride was going to be about you getting stronger and enjoying this beautiful scenery. Instead, you go deep, you look forward, and you are one strong cookie."

She laughed and so did he. "Thanks, I'm trying."

"Look, my original mom was beautiful on the outside and evil on the inside, so I'm looking for beauty on the *inside*, and you are full of it and I already know, we're going to be a good team."

Her heart filled. "I agree, now, if I can only make that beautiful lady riding on that horse behind us know she doesn't have to worry about me anymore, that she's brought me exactly where I'm supposed to be. If she realizes that, *maybe* she can move forward with her life."

Wes nodded. "Yup, I agree. Just between you and me, since we are going to be riding this path a lot together, trying to help anybody who needs us. I'm hoping Nick gets what I see in his eyes when he looks at your sister."

Rainy's heart swelled. "You're right. We see a lot of things alike because as much as my amazing sister doesn't want to see it too, I'm rooting for those two."

# CHAPTER SIXTEEN

After they had ridden a little while Emmy knew without a doubt that this was the right choice for her sister. Her sister was smiling. Pretty much all the time. Watching her ride beside big strong Wes filled her with joy.

Seeing Rainy telling Tony hello when they got back to the ranch, and there he sat on the tailgate of his old work truck watching for them. Wes grinned at him and Emmy was glad she and her horse were in a position so that she could see the reactions. There was no strain between the two young men because as she'd watched Rainy ride beside Wes, she had sensed that there was a bond between them but not an attraction. But it was clear that in Tony's eyes there was an attraction to Rainy and the same for him from Rainy. Her smile down at him when he strode to her to help her off the horse was clear. She was so glad to see him.

Wes nonchalantly walked away to the walker as Tony carefully eased her sister from the saddle into his arms then their gazes locked as he turned and carried her to where Wes, eyes twinkling Wes, waiting with the walker.

Heart thundering, Emmy looked at Nick, sure enough by the look in his eyes he too knew that something was connecting Rainy and Tony.

Unable to keep her attention on that she gave her horse a little touch with her knee and he moved forward to the fence. She was a little rattled by what she'd just seen, her sister was attracted to Tony. Her sister had no qualms or fears about it. She, on the other hand, lived with all of that. She pulled her leg over the horse, her thoughts kicking around in her head. When she went to step down from the stirrup she didn't pull her boot out as needed. Instantly she fell backwards.

"Ugg," she gasped, but to her startled surprise she landed in the arms of Nick.

"Gotcha." When I saw you start to dismount, I hopped down from my horse and came over just in case." He grinned, that amazing, enticing curl of his lips.

Her heart swirled, just being in his arms, safe, close against him, his heart pounding against hers. And those amazing cinnamon eyes dug deep into hers. Time paused, her heart thundered and all she felt besides the thundering heart was the peace he sent through her. And the need to have more of this feeling this man sent to her with just a look and a smile.

"Thank you," she said, her words more of a mumble than clearly spoken, bringing a wider grin to his face. It just turned her insides into pandemonium.

"I've been looking for an excuse to get close to you and you gave it to me. So, thanks."

She chuckled, a laugh escaped her and the twinkle in his eyes made her happy. "I guess I needed to repay you for the joy today has brought me. Rainy had a wonderful day, it's obvious. And I owe that to you. Thank you for doing this. Your ranch—rehabilitation ranch—not sure what you're going to call it. But I'm going to call it a miracle ranch. A place where not just physical achievements can be made, but heart stopping, life-changing miracles for those involved."

His arm that was below her legs, wrapped beneath and around her knees and the one that was around her back with his hand around her shoulder tightened. Only then did she realize she was still in his arms. Still being held as if she was a treasure—something she'd never thought she wanted from a man.

Something she'd never thought she'd need.

Something she'd never thought she'd want.

"I think I *need* to stand on my own two feet," she said, her words solid, thank goodness. Her brain had sprung back from where it had gone.

Again, this was not about her, but Rainy. And that was something she knew now she was going to have to remind herself of, harder and more determined because this cowboy was dangerous to her goals.

No matter how powerful and wonderful; attracting, heart-pumping, emotion-filled feelings he caused her, this was not where she wanted to go!

She clarified the last word with an exclamation mark and a determined edge. And thank goodness he set her on her feet. Her unsteady feet. He held her arm, thank goodness, making sure she was steady as if he saw in her eyes how affected she was by him.

"I think we better go get this rodeo going again, I mean this great day for your sister." Then his hand dropped from her shoulder and he started walking toward Rainy, Wes, and to an overjoyed, smiling Tony who had just set her sister on her feet and she was holding the rungs of her walker smiling at Emmy.

Oh goodness what a day this had been.

* * *

Nick worked hard that evening after the horse ride with Rainy and Emmy. He'd been able to hold everything inside as he'd gone over and told Rainy and Wes that they'd done a great job. He'd encouraged Rainy to keep up the good work. That the riding and the steadiness she was building in her upper torso and her legs, getting the rhythm in with the horse as he walked beneath her. It would help her walk without her walker one day.

To his surprise Rainy had smiled. Then said, "I'll walk but one thing I can promise you is that riding is providing me with stability in my mind and soul. Providing me with goals and a desire in me to help others. I talked with Wes on the ride and I know where I'm going now. I'm going to do like Wes and Tony." She smiled at both guys. "I'm going to make this my mission. My goal. To help others like you're doing. When I came here to live with my sister, it was just with the goal to share life with her again. But she had chosen this wonderful place with all you amazing fellas and those astonishing, lovely people from town. God had a hand in all of this and I see it. So, get ready because we're going to push it. We're going to push it to the limits with me. We're going to learn using me, what and how much we can do to push for it. So, I am happy at the first learning experience of this wonderful place…and we're going to change lives."

Her words still rang inside of him. His heart swelled just thinking about them. He knew exactly what she had seen almost from her first moment on that horse's back. Something he hadn't seen when he'd first come here to the foster home that had become his family. He'd been too caught up in trying to make something of his life that would get back at the people that had thrown him out like a piece of wadded up trash and left him there on the side of the road. He wanted to get back at them as an adult. That had been his driving force—but Rainy, beautiful inside and out Rainy, didn't look back.

She didn't look over her shoulder at what had happened to her and want to get back at the scum who had done this to her. Wes had taken his anger and his looking back out on those raging bulls but he'd come back here. Like him, Wes had realized that what he was doing wasn't giving him any satisfaction. But then there was Tony…

Tony, like Rainy, hadn't looked back. He'd always looked forward. Always strove to help others and never sought to leave this place he called home.

He always looked at what he could do, how he could help everyone around him. All the boys knew this. And she wanted to know more.

* * *

The week after the ride on the ranch, when Emmy hadn't gotten off her horse by herself and Nick had caught her in his powerful arms, she couldn't get him out of her mind or off her heart. She worked at the store on Monday, thankful it was busy, helping a bit to distract her from Nick.

Then, he came by on Monday afternoon and told her he'd be gone that week and not be back until late Saturday. That meant there wouldn't be any riding, unless they wanted to come out and ride with Wes. She'd been relieved when Rainy told her she would work on her stability on the bars on the back porch and spend time with Tony, Wes, and Caleb in Caleb's shop during the day, so riding wasn't a priority. They were sharing ideas and working on things to help others like her ride horses.

That meant Emmy spent most of the week working in her shop with customers coming and going, and a lot of time in the afternoon alone... her mind stuck on Nick. Afraid the ladies would see something was wrong, she'd stayed away from the diner too.

Then last night, she and Rainy had a deep talk and her world was spinning and thankfully it was Friday, Flora's day to work. God's timing was right because Emmy needed something space, needed a quiet place to think.

A place to run away to and so she did. She ran to the place that called her... *Nick's ranch.*

He wasn't supposed to be back until the next day so she headed out for time alone. Feeling some relief as she drove toward his ranch, knowing there was a wonderful lake partially visible from the road and it drew her. It looked like the perfect place for much needed time alone.

Yes, she knew Nick's ranch drew her because of him but also because it was a place that would be for hurting people to get help, to achieve new goals inside and out and at the moment that was her.

She drove through the entrance and then onto the side road that angled from his driveway and led to the gate to the pasture surrounding the lake. She hopped from her SUV and hurried to free the chain that latched it to the fence post. Then she pushed the gate open and all the way back to latch it to the other post that held it open for cattle to pass through or trucks... or a woman looking for peace. Finally, she drove her SUV through it, quickly got out, closed it again then drove to the lake.

She sighed loudly, alone in her cab as the peaceful lake came into view. It was beautiful, peaceful and very much needed.

She scrambled from the SUV then strode to the water's edge as quick as she could there and stood with her hand to her rapid beating heart as she took it all in. It was picturesque, especially close up, the water was calm, and the sun glistened on it. She breathed in the fresh air and let her shoulders relax. She was so glad she'd come.

Along the water's edge there were thin trails, and since living in the area she'd seen, in many of the acres of pastures, cattle walking along trails like this. But always at a distance, so this was her first close up. She studied the small trail made from cow hooves that obviously stepped almost footstep to footstep keeping the trails thin but well-traveled. Perfect for walking by herself—just dodging a splash of dried cow patties along the way—the same as life. That comparison actually brought a smile to her lips, then a much-needed chuckle.

Unable to help herself, she put her hands in her

pockets and looked down at her leather boots, good walking shoes in this area. And so she walked along the edge of the lake, following the trails, dodging cow patties. Not too often, but enough to know that today she was lucky because the cows had left the lake alone just for her.

Could the cow patties of her life do the same?

The trail split into two, one continuing along the water's edge and one going up a two-foot hill then, continuing around the lake just like the one parallel to it next to the water. When the area from the lake to the pasture grew deeper, there was a third trail along the upper ridge. She stayed in the middle trail, liking that she was close to the water but giving a little distance and a picturesque, calming view from the few feet above.

Like her, the cattle trails told that some cows preferred low, some high, and those like her somewhere in the middle. She wondered if that was something to do with her approach to life all together...

Staying in the middle, safe with boundary lines above and below. She paused as that thought slammed into her—*am I too much in the middle?*

Rainy had quickly known what path she was taking, and it was on an avenue of discovery and recovery—but her own way. Emmy stood there on the center lane—frozen suddenly. Three choices and she chose the middle. She pushed the strange tugging thought away and continued walking the center trail. She could see across the water, across the pasture and when she turned and looked behind her, she could see past the upper trail and the far-reaching land spread out around her. The middle trail was the perfect trail. Safe.

*Yes, but right?*

She looked back across the water, her heart pounding as she continued walking, then suddenly the center trail led only upward. Up the ravine to the upper trail, and she had no choice but to follow it or turn back. She took the higher trail and then stopped and gazed across the beautiful lake, then down at the area below her as the breeze picked up and tossed her hair about her shoulders. It was a beautiful sight.

Calm enveloped her, a refreshing feeling. Just what she needed. She needed calmness desperately. Her whole life had been a rioting, worried experience. Yes, she'd calmed some when she'd moved here, knowing that she was going to give her sister a new start in this wonderful place. But in this moment, as she looked around and the beautiful sunshine on the horizon glistened as soft blue mingled with gold and orange streaks, beautiful but her gaze rested on the many trails through the pasture. She could see from where she now stood on the higher level, trails through the green pastures that had led many cows from fresh feed to the water and a drink to replenish them. The picture was vivid in her mind.

Here she stood on the trail that had led her to looking out over this beautiful, peaceful sanctuary...she breathed deeply and smiled. A sanctuary was what she'd needed and here she stood. Her gaze went to the lake and the gorgeous reflection of the sun shining in it like a golden welcoming sign. It enveloped her—se should be happy. Her sister had told her as they sat on the porch last night that she was from now on only moving forward, never looking back. Why, because she was in exactly the spot she was supposed to be in. *This* was the turning point of her life.

"Emmy, I can use my life to help others take steps forward and hopefully embrace their future, striving to make it as wonderful and beneficial to others as possible." Rainy's voice had trembled with emotion. "I didn't die, or suffer before that because Emmy, you protected me." Then she'd continued talking about others, like Tony, who had suffered immensely. Wes too, but Tony had lived a life of helping everybody around him. He would remain in Dew Drop on Sunrise Ranch. Rainy had said the words smiling, then her sweet eyes glistened with tears. "He's planning to bring beautiful sunrises to every boy who comes here from despicable backgrounds to start over." Rainy had wiped her eyes as she locked gazes with Emmy. "Tony *never* looks back. He never asks why."

The words stuck in Emmy's heart as Rainy said she asked him one night when they were outside their barn while Caleb was inside building a new wheelchair application, she'd asked him why he didn't want to talk about his background and what had happened to him?

He'd said, "The scars on my back aren't of my making, but now that I had them they are for me to make what good I can from them."

Emmy stared across the water and placed her hand over her trembling lips as the scene continued to play out in her mind. Rainy, her dear sister had wiped her eyes, stood up, leaned over and given Emmy a hug. And while doing it she'd let go of her walker and did it all on her own balance and strength.

Then, she'd actually straightened on her own and for a moment of her strength she'd stood there smiling down at Emmy before taking hold of the handlebars. "Sister, it's time for us to only move forward. Don't look back, *Don't* think about me. I'm happy. You got me here. *You* brought me to my destiny. Those are the words Tony told me after I'd asked him again to tell me what he'd been through. He said, "What happened to me was bad. But it brought me here to Dew Drop and Sunrise Ranch, to my destiny. He placed his hand on my shoulder, smiled at me and told me he felt it was the same for me. And *oh*, Emmy, it is. I'm happy. I'm going to do everything I can to walk straighter, but if I can't it's okay. I'm happy. And you found this wonderful place for me. You did. Now, I want you to let me go and to find your own happiness. Stop looking back. Just stop. You deserve a have a happy future too."

And then her sister had walked away leaving Emmy sitting there alone, her world spiraling around her. Tears welled up then and now as Emmy wiped them from her cheeks, took a deep, shaky breath. Her sweet sister had smiled at her and today standing here on the ridge of the lake, heart throbbing, Emmy was still thinking about that moment.

That moment she'd watched her sister push her walker down the path along the trail with spunky-bright toned flowers beside her and she'd been softly humming all the way. She was happy. Satisfied.

Now, Emmy wrapped her arms around herself and held on tight, her shoulders trembled and emotion she hadn't felt in so long erupted inside of her. Tears streamed down her cheeks as she let go of anxiety and anger she'd held back for so very long and she let herself cry while standing there on that beautiful hillside surrounded by open fields.

Could she look at this like her life was now open?

Could she let go and not look back on what had driven her for so long?

Could she face life like her sister was doing?

# CHAPTER SEVENTEEN

Nicholas drove in through the entrance of his ranch, startled to have seen Emmy at the lake. Standing on the lake's far side, on the upper ridge, she stood still and stunning with the setting sun casting light across the lake and over her too. Like a beacon in the light, she glowed and his heart instantly shot into a rampant rhythm.

She was too far away so he couldn't see her emotions but she was there and by the stance she stood at, her shoulders curved forward, her arms wrapped around her waist, she looked emotional. His heart raced from just seeing her here on his land but also with worry—*was she okay?*

He immediately drove his truck toward the lake,

jumped out and opened the gate then moments later, leaving the gate wide open he drove across the pasture with one destination before him. Emmy.

Ignoring the road because it went to the lake on this side and she'd walked the trails around to the far side so he drove straight across the pasture. It was rough from cow tracks and possum holes, he bumped along and ignored the thump to his head on the ceiling when he hit a dirt mound at high speed.

His focus on Emmy and only Emmy.

He wanted to get to her, to see if everything was okay.

All week he'd missed her as he'd gone to another ranch on the far side of Texas to see how they handled helping kids with their problems. It had been inspiring and had helped him know more about what he was going to do. He'd gotten on his laptop computer and ordered a lot of things he would need. And he had, as of now, officially opened.

His lawyer had taken care of all the legal work and now he was happy to know that the *Forward Moving Ranch of No Regrets* was officially opened.

It was a long name but one he'd adopted from Tony's mind. The boy only moved forward and regretted nothing because it put him where he felt he should be. And that was where Nicholas wanted to be and everyone who came to the ranch when they headed back home.

And his new friend, the owner at the other ranch was happy to have him on board because he knew there were more out there who could use the help they offered on the backs of their beloved horses and open pastureland.

And the beauty standing on the hillside before him. Nicholas pulled to a hard stop, rushed from his truck then stood there staring up the path that led to Emmy. He prayed with all his heart that there was a future between them.

Hope for them.

She'd turned as he'd driven across the pasture and now she stood there looking across the land separating them. His heart raced realizing her eyes glisten with tears. Forcing himself to walk quickly but still walk, not race up the hillside, his heart pounded with each step. Pounding harder every step closer he got to her. Then as he drew near she stepped toward him.

*Do not overdo this.*

The voice in his head had to make the demand because he knew this woman that he'd only held in his arms a few times had taken over his heart. He stopped two steps away from her.

She took another step toward him. "Nick, I needed to see you and you appeared. God has a way…"

He grinned. "Oh yes, He does. I needed to see you too."

She took a breath. "Rainy told me she was never looking back. That she was taking Tony's advice and moving forward like he has done. And she told me point blank that I need to stop looking back and step forward too. That's basically what she said before she walked away, pushing her walker, singing as she went—oh Nick she's so happy. And that makes me happy," she said, her voice trembling.

"But it's hard on you, right?" His *world* trembled.

"Yes. I don't know how to feel about that. I feel bad that it confuses me so."

"Maybe she knows it's time for you to move

forward. I had that moment when I realized, despite making all the money I made I wasn't moving forward. I was overhauling ruined businesses I bought and getting them back on track for resale but not my own life. With the right money and the right people, selling them for a good profit it should have been rewarding in more than just dollars. But to me, it wasn't. In my own life I hadn't put the wrong on the back burner or on the burn pile. I hadn't put *myself* on the track to change but had stayed on the wrong track that came from my past that I'd never let go of... I hadn't put everything where it needed to be. It took coming back here the last couple of years, seeing the changes going on with my brothers for it to hit home. Seeing the happiness they'd found moving forward in their lives, finding love and fulfilment giving back to the younger brothers."

He couldn't help it, he lifted his hand and gently touched her cheek. Then let his fingers take the strand of warn brown hair that was caught on her lip and he pulled it away then let his hand rest on her shoulder. She didn't move away, and that made his heart sing.

"And that included my sister," she breathed out.

"Yes, it was meant to be. I knew I had to not just

make a difference with money in my life, I needed to make a difference in other people's lives. And I hoped—even prayed, that at some point the right woman would come along and I'd be as happy as my brothers. You can look at them and see that they radiate happiness. Them and their wonderful wives. Their love radiates to these boys. The boys who are just as happy for them as they would have been if their lives hadn't had such hardships involved. They too, get excited about happy-ever-afters. How about you?"

She stared at him and he saw in her beautiful caramel toned eyes happy-ever-after brought a glow of hope. It was a flash, but it had been there. If only it was an everlasting adventure she could step out and take with him.

He pushed on. "Yeah, it's hard, isn't it? The stepping out. That risk that you've been afraid of. Emmy, you watched your parents go through a lot of bad things. Giving into alcoholism and you experienced their abuse. But *you*, strong woman that you are, protected your little sister with everything you had. And when she was hurt, it tore you up inside. You, sweet Emmy Swanson, are an amazing, wonderful woman.

You're willing to put your life on hold, spend all these years to find the right place to bring your sister to live when you and she were reunited. And you have wonderful vision because you picked exactly the right place. But how about you? Are you ready to step out like she is and claim your new life?"

\* \* \*

This man, this man she *loved*, his words sank deep and Emmy wanted to throw herself into his arms…but she couldn't make mistakes.

Oh she knew he wasn't a mistake, but she came from two terrible people and they left scars on her body, never anything like Tony's but still her back showed scars. Scars that had long ago healed, but they were still alive in her heart. "I hid my pain in my love for my sister. Thinking about her pain and stopping it helped me not think about mine. And I," her words broke as tears once again welled up inside of her. In that moment the man who had the potential to change her life stepped in and wrapped his strong arms around her. Once again, her head rested on his shoulder and her arms wrapped around him. She clung tight to him, breathing in his scent, his heart, the man that he was to her.

"Darlin', let it out. Just let it loose. Let. It. Go. There is *nothing*, not one thing about your past that you can change. The only thing you can change is how it affects you. Yes, you escaped it by helping your sister, but your sister overcame partly because she's one tough little gal, and a sweetheart, but also because she watched you. She saw how you fought to help her overcome and to make a place for her to come live with you.

"She watched you fight and take hideous acts of violence while you made her hide for her safety's sake. That smart girl loves you with all of her heart, she just has one hope now that she's found her place and that's that you will step out and like you fought for her, now fight for yourself. Are you going to fight, Emmy?"

His words next to her ear, his breath raking through her as she trembled in his arms, radiated so much and she knew, yes, letting go was something she *had* to do. She pulled her head back and looked him in the eyes, his warm cinnamon eyes. Her eyes were on equal level to his tempting lips, the lips she wished to kiss but she focused on his eyes, eyes that beckoned her to freedom.

*Freedom.* "Nick, I don't want to lead you on—"

"You're not leading me on. I'm already there," he said, a hint of humor in his words. "Emmy, I can't stop thinking about you. I can't go to sleep without thinking about holding you in my arms when you're happy, not just when your sad and crying, like now. Emmy, I want to be the man who shows you that life can be beautiful, wonderful, and happy. Forevermore. Because honestly, since the day I walked into the Cow Patty Café and sat down at that table and heard your sweet voice—then you looked at me, my life has never been the same. *You* have brought my future into the spotlight. But I can't force that on you. You may not feel for me what I feel for you—"

Emmy cut his words off, unable to stop herself, she lifted to her toes and met his lips with hers. Her arms squeezed tightly as his instantly did the same. He kissed her, with a deep, deep love that she felt from the top of her head to the tips of her toes. In that instant she knew she'd never dreamed of anything so wonderful. This man, *this man,* was her happily ever after.

# CHAPTER EIGHTEEN

*He was in heaven.*

Nickolas had the woman of his dreams, holding her close and he wanted to drop to his knee—but didn't know if now was the time to go down on his knee and ask her to marry him. They hadn't even been on a date. They'd just taken this step forward, hopefully toward a new life, a life together. He pulled his lips away, cupped her face with his hands and smiled at her.

He'd be smiling for the rest of his life. "Emmy, I love you. I know we've not known each other for long but this is more for me than just holding you and kissing you. I don't want to rush this. You have a lot going on in your life with your sister and well…getting used to me. So, right now I want to ask you out, since we haven't been on a date. Will you go on a date with me?"

A smile spread across her face. "You're probably right, this shouldn't be rushed. But you should know that I'm serious."

He kissed the top of her nose. "I'm very serious too, about a future with you and about a date. We need to have an official date. Something we haven't been on. Two people fall in love…I'm assuming you love me."

"Yes, you're one smart cowboy. So, when are you taking me on this date?"

"Tomorrow after church we're supposed to ride with Rainy and Wes. But, I'm thinking that they wouldn't mind if we kept the ride short and—no, that won't work. I think we'll wait till Monday. I would say Friday or Saturday but I can't wait that long. I want to take you to dinner out of town, just you and me and show you that I'm not just a cowboy on a ranch riding a horse all the time."

She reached up and cupped his hands that were still touching her face and she pulled them down between them. Their clasped hands were now touching his heart and her shoulder—he was a little taller than her and that was okay. "I want to go to dinner with you too. You know, take that step forward and have fun. Really, it's a very good idea. I'm excited thinking about it. Honestly, Nick, I've never been on a date."

He stepped back, slapped with shock unable to believe it. "Seriously, *you*—never?"

She lifted her shoulders. "No, attention has always been elsewhere, on my sister and then trying to figure out what I was going to do to make life right for her. I've never really even been tempted to go on a date. I was raised by a maniac after all."

"True and I'm sorry. But," he said, a big grin splashed across his face and his heart. "I'm the man who is going to show you there is more. You should know I've been on dates but never have I been so excited about a date—the other are wiped away just thinking about you. Never have I ever been on a date with a woman I was in love with, or saw a future with. So, Monday evening I'm picking you up and we're going to have a special evening."

"That means I have to tell a few people…I guess."

He lifted his finger of his right hand to her jaw. "If

you want to. Whatever you want. I'd shout it to the world but only if you're ready for that."

She looked a bit nervous. "I think I need to tell Rainy. I'll do that tonight and then, I'm not sure. Now that I'm getting to know the spirit in that sister of mine more, she's going to be excited and she might shout it to the world. Is that okay with you?"

"Emmy, let me make this clear." In that moment, unable to stop himself he dropped to his knee there on the hill overlooking the lake with the sun setting on the horizon. Holding her hand in his, he said, "Emmy Swanson, never in my life have I ever, ever loved anyone, other than my brothers and no one like I love you. So, Emmy, will you marry me? This is just between you and me, and then we will go from there at your pace. I thought about doing it on our dinner date on Monday but—" He chuckled. "If you turn me down I'll be here waiting, praying that you don't just walk away."

Emmy's hand tightened on his, her hand trembled and those eyes, those beautiful golden eyes of hers had tears in them as she looked down on him. "Nick, I'd never walk away. I've waited all of my life for you—

without even knowing I was doing it. Yes, I'll marry you. I love you, I'm going to be Mrs. Emmy McDermott, and nothing has ever sounded so perfect to me."

Nick rose, swung her up into his arms, loving the feel of her as he spun around on the hillside. His heart was as high as the skyline. "This is more than I ever expected. More than I ever dreamed of." And then, he kissed her again.

And would kiss her for the rest of his life.

* * *

Emmy and Nick had told everyone the next day at church. The day after they'd opened their hearts to each other and were now planning a wedding. Even before they went on their first date. They told their wonderful news and instantly everyone had enveloped them in hugs and cheers.

The next evening, her sister was so excited that she'd helped Emmy get dressed for her date. She'd wore a beautiful dress from her store. Soft blue with a flowing skirt and a pair of heels. She had no idea where they were going but she dressed like she felt, uplifted and happy like a blue horizon. And Rainy, bless her loving heart had totally agreed.

And the date.

Oh, the date had been as wonderful and romantic as she'd dreamed.

Nick had gone out of his way to give her the most romantic first date of her life. They'd driven to one of the many scenic, lovely restaurants that could be found along the, sometimes rough but loved, Blanco River. They'd driven a little further from Dew Drop to one almost to Wimberly. It was worth the drive. Of course being in the truck with Nick made it worth driving forever. The lovely restaurant with a table on the far end of the deck overlooking some rapids and a beautiful sunset. They'd enjoyed time together, sometimes laughing, eating the wonderful food, but most of all just being with him and not worrying at that moment about anything.

It had been amazing.

She knew there would be times in normal life that

she would have those times but not being worried about her sister for the first time in her life had been a relief. But also, realizing that deep down inside of herself there had been a knot of tension, of worry about her own life. And she'd released it, totally and completely. That night they'd lifted their glasses of lemon ice water and toasted to a wonderful future together. She'd asked him then the question that had been burning inside of her.

"Do you want children?"

His gaze had dug deep. "I want children. I want *our* children. I want our lives to be mixed together through our love and our children—but only if you want them. And if for some reason that I'm not yet aware of, and there isn't a possibility of that, then I want to adopt children. Boys or girls like me who need a home to be loved in. Adoption is always open."

Oh what a man. "Well," she'd said. "I want children of my own with you or adopted. I'm all in, whereever our hearts and life take us. We might end up having a humongous home." A smile bloomed across her face and heart.

He'd grinned widely then placed his hand over hers

and squeezed gently. "We will go at it one at a time. One thing I know for certain is our children will be loved and cherished. They'll know we love them like Morgan, Tucker, and Rowdy knew when they lost their mother to cancer. Not because she'd thrown them aside or just been unable to take care of them, but because she'd left them with her love in their hearts and with amazing Randolph and Nana to carry on her love. So, we will limit ourselves on our family size. But in *our* dream, I'm calling it that since you're in on it too..." He'd grinned and she had too, loving the man with everything in her. "We're going to open this ranch with the dream of helping others like Rainy, loving them to a stronger capability in maneuvering life, physically and mentally."

And that was why she loved him. Yes, as happy as she was feeling, she wanted to love the world but she needed the security of a home built for her and the children they would share. And then the world was open with bringing kids in who needed them to help find a steady life. Like her sister was doing.

And so, that had been their date and today, as she

stood at the counter in her store, the door opened and the man of her dreams poked his good-looking head inside and smiled.

Then drawled, "Howdy, you amazing woman, are you ready to go to the Cow Patty Café for lunch?"

Her heart roared. "*Yes*, I am," she said, her words rolling out on a laugh of love. "This is so wonderful—I love that diner. I love everyone in it, but now I'm going to love it more because I'm going with you." She walked across the room and into his arms and planted a quick kiss on his smiling lips then headed out the open door. He pulled it shut and she locked it.

He took her hand in his and they headed down the sidewalk and of course Drewbaker and Chili whistled at the same time.

Nick slowed their pace. "You boys are always nice to see."

"Not as great as it is to finally see you two together," Drewbaker said.

"And that is the truth," Chili added. "That day Emmy came here, before going inside and telling the ladies she was bringing Rainy to town, was a special day. Then you drove up and we told you about it, and you went in that diner—that was a great day. We knew from that day forward that you two were meant to be together. We just kept it to ourselves."

"Yes, we did," Drewbaker said. "We knew it from almost the first moment—not that we're matchmakers," he finished and hitched an eyebrow.

"But, sometimes we get the sense of things," Chili halfway grunted and laughed.

Emmy knew it seemed to be true. These two fellas sat here on this bench and watched everyone come and go. Suddenly it slammed into her—the other thing that had been on her mind since the day standing there on the side of the hill listening to Edwina. "So, do you watch everyone?"

"*Yee*up," Chili said with a twang and both he and Drewbaker grinned.

"Then do *y'all* know who might be interested in Edwina?"

Both of them leaned back, cocked their heads to the side as if the same puppeteer was controlling their heads with strings, and they stayed that way for a moment.

Yes, she knew just by that action and their fake quizzical looks on their faces. "Y'all do know who this mystery man is," she gushed. Excitement filled her.

Drewbaker sat the carving he'd been holding on his knee and the hand holding his knife on his other knee. "Well, we've never been sure but we do know that there is one tall, broad-shouldered cowboy who *never* misses a day in that diner. Of course there have been a few days when we weren't sitting here in our seats so he might have missed a day. But he's a steady man in there and out of there."

"*And*," Chili broke in. "He's always in a boot-stomping hurry to get in there and walking slow when he leaves."

Wow. "So, who is it?"

Chili grinned and looked at his friend who hitched his thick eyebrow. Drewbaker shook his head. "Darlin'," Chili then said. "We don't always tell everything. We just watch and then if we need to step in and do a little manipulating when the time is needed or right, we might just do that."

"Like you know," Drewbaker broke in. "Taking

that determined sister of yours out on that tin cup ride with those two young cowboys who are both going to be great men one day. And well, we just want to help people take the steps they need to head in the right direction."

She looked at Nick, who was grinning. "I have to agree with them. I'm glad they didn't, you know, step in and try to get in mine and your business. But now that I think about what they did for Tony, Wes, and Rainy, I think they know what they're doing. So, I'm good with that." She drilled her eyes to them. "But now that you've got my curiosity up I'm going to be watching for this Edwina admirer. I may have to start taking lessons from you two—though I'm not going to sit on that bench for the rest of my life like y'all do."

"Hey," Chili yelped. "We worked our whole lives. Now we enjoy sittin' here carving these pretty little pieces of wooden animals and giving them away."

"Yep," Drewbaker added. "We like being birds in a tree and watching everything going on around us."

Emmy laughed and so did Nick. "Well then, I'll let it be, but I'm going to be on the lookout too. I'm having the happily ever after with the man of my life and I've always felt drawn to Edwina. She's got her thoughts on maybe taking a step forward like I did, so I'm doing nothing to interrupt that. Okay, so let's go to lunch." She grinned at the two of them and then tugged Nick forward.

"Sounds like a perfect plan," Nick agreed, tipping his hat at the two watching, grinning men.

They walked the last few steps, while Drewbaker and Chili chuckled, then Nick pulled open the bright yellow door, they stepped inside, the cow started mooing, and there was Edwina.

She walked up, looking from her to Nick. Instantly, a huge grin spread across the waitress's face. Edwina usually had a stern, stand-back look to her and a grim line of lips that told everyone to mind their own business and straighten up or else. But, right now her happy smile lit up everything on her face telling Emmy how delighted she was to see her and Nick together. Her friends delight sent a powerful blast of love through Emmy.

Instantly Emmy wrapped her arms around Edwina

like Nick had done that day. "I'm so excited to see you, Edwina, and there is something I have to ask you right here in the middle of this diner and I mean it with all of my heart. When me and this handsome cowboy get married I need a maid of honor and I want you—if you would do me the honor."

Edwina leaned back, shock on her face. "*Seriously?*"

Emmy nodded. "Completely serious. Never been more serious about anything in my life, beside loving Rainy and this man standing beside me. The man I know loves you too."

Edwina jerked her head one way and then the other, taking in everyone in the room and then she grinned even wider. "Well, I think that'll be an honor. I mean, life changes doesn't it, my dear friend?"

"Yes, it does if we open our hearts and…watch for the right man." Her heart raged as she met Edwina's eyes straight on.

Edwina nodded. "I agree. So, yes, you tell me when, what in the world to wear, and if I have to wear heels—oh my goodness gracious I haven't worn those in a very, *very* long time."

The room had been silent as everyone watched, now laughter erupted. Edwina whirled around and though Emmy couldn't see her eyes she knew Edwina was shooting a glare around the room at everyone who was so happy.

But now stopping it, there were smiles across everyone's faces along with Miss Jo, and then big amazing T-bone, with his chef apron on, came out to stand beside Miss Jo, a wide grin on his face too.

Edwina stared them all down. "Now, don't y'all go gettin' any ideas. I'm serious about this. I'll do what this sweet lady wants me to do. Even wear heels if I need to—and a dress. *But*, don't go getting any ideas that I'll be wearing anything dressier here than this outfit I have on right now. My jeans, my belt—which I can whip off real fast if I need to get anyone straight—and my white shirt. You got it?"

"Sure," or similar agreements everyone said.

And then Nick wrapped his right arm around Emmy and his left arm around Edwina and he kissed her on the temple. "Girl, I am glad you're going to join in on our wedding and be the maid of honor. And I can't wait to see you in those heels and that dress. I've got a feelin' there's going to be a *lot* of cowboys at our wedding now."

Emmy hugged him tight and looked at Edwina. "I have a feeling he's right. And that makes me happy."

Edwina grinned. "Well, I told you I been having thoughts of making changes in my life because of that darlin' sister of yours, and now you've stepped in and given me more motivation. So, with my mind on straight I might just take a chance—no, I *will* take a chance."

Emmy cheered, everyone cheered and at the back of the room, Larson—big, tall Larson, jumped up slapping his hands hard together and knocked his table over, it slammed to the floor bringing all attention to him. And the look of shock on his face. It was as though he hadn't even noticed what he'd done, because his eyes were locked on Edwina as his large hands continued slamming together, clapping with powerful enthusiasm.

Everyone else paused, gapping at the excited cowboy.

Edwina instantly stepped away from Emmy and

Nick slapped her hands to her hips. "Time to calm down. Come on, sit." She waved her hands indicating to sit. "Everybody just sit, sit, sit. And *you*, cowboy, grab another table and I'll clean that mess up—gives me a good reason to get back to work. I'll bring you another plate."

With that Edwina stomped to the kitchen as everyone did as she demanded. But they were all grinning.

Emmy's gaze was locked on Larson, had she seen exactly what she'd thought she'd seen? He had not moved at first, his gaze had followed Edwina to the kitchen and now, he spun toward the table, grabbed it by the edges and had it on its legs in an instant. Then the two chairs were back in place and as Edwina came back from the kitchen carrying the broom.

Miss Jo and a smiling T-bone headed back to the kitchen—she could see Miss Jo's grin before she turned then disappeared behind the swinging doors and knew she was thinking exactly like Emmy. Larson had it bad.

*Real bad*.

The man had obviously been waiting for the

moment Edwina let down her walls.

Emmy was thrilled when Edwina slowed her strides, seeing what Larson had done and now he was on one knee on the floor picking up the pieces of a broken dish.

*Could he be the man to pick up the pieces of Edwina's broken heart?*

"What are yo—" Edwina said but halted when Larson looked up at her, still on one knee and an arm resting on the other.

His eyes were kind and seeking—"I've got this," he said, gently but firmly with a smile to finish it off. "If you'll hand me that broom I'll clean up my own mess, but will be happy to have a replacement of my meal, if you don't mind."

Frozen in place Edwina didn't move for a minute, then she slowly held the broom out to him and his smile widened. And his eyes twinkled.

*Twinkled.*

"Thank you. You are one *amazing* lady."

"Um, I gotta get your food," Edwina said, spun and her eyes met Emmy's and there was a sudden side hitch to Edwina's lips. Then she stormed to the kitchen.

Stunned and excited Emmy had to hold back a huge grin that flashed through her as she spun toward a smiling Nick. The last thing they needed was to mess this up for Edwina. Nick got it and instantly, together they headed toward an empty table in the opposite direction of the hopefully about to bloom romance.

This was just wonderful, she now knew exactly who to watch. She was certain she knew who had *hopes* for a date with Edwina. And she wasn't the only one. It was all up to wonderful Edwina now—and she was ready.

But right now, Emmy focused on the man walking with her to the table, hand in hand. The amazing man she planned to be with for the rest of her life.

Her story she knew had a great happily-ever-after to it. And because of that…Emmy was the happiest woman in the world.

*Hopefully, Edwina would soon be as blessed as she was*

# More Books in the Series

## Cowboys of Dew Drop, Texas

Unforgettable Cowboy (Book 1)

Unexpected Cowboy (Book 2)

Unlikely Cowboy (Book 3)

Undeniable Cowboy (Book 4)

Undisputable Cowboy (Book 5)

## Check out Debra's Other Series

Texas Matchmakers At It Again

Star Gazer Inn of Corpus Christi Bay

Sunset Bay Romance

Texas Brides & Bachelors

New Horizon Ranch Series

Turner Creek Ranch Series

Cowboys of Ransom Creek

Texas Matchmaker Series

Windswept Bay Series

# About the Author

Debra Clopton is a USA Today bestselling & International bestselling author who has sold over 3.5 million books. She has published over 81 books under her name and her pen name of Hope Moore.

Under both names she writes clean & wholesome and inspirational, small town romances, especially with cowboys but also loves to sweep readers away with romances set on beautiful beaches surrounded by topaz water and romantic sunsets.

Her books now sell worldwide and are regulars on the Bestseller list in the United States and around the world. Debra is a multiple award-winning author, but of all her awards, it is her reader's praise she values most. If she can make someone smile and forget their worries for a few hours (or days when binge reading one of her series) then she's done her job and her heart is happy. She really loves hearing she kept a reader from doing the dishes or sleeping!

A sixth-generation Texan, Debra lives on a ranch in Texas with her husband surrounded by cattle, deer, very busy squirrels and hole digging wild hogs. She enjoys traveling and spending time with her family.

Visit Debra's website and sign up for her newsletter
for updates at: www.debraclopton.com

Check out her Facebook at:
www.facebook.com/debra.clopton.5

Follow her on Instagram at: debraclopton_author

or contact her at debraclopton@ymail.com

Printed in the USA
CPSIA information can be obtained
at www.ICGtesting.com
LVHW052307170424
777752LV00037B/1199